By

Virgil E. Scott,
Keith E. Evans,
David R. Patton,
Charles P. Stone,

PREFACE

This Handbook is the result of a cooperative effort between the Forest Service, U.S. Department of Agriculture, and the Fish and Wildlife Service, U.S. Department of the Interior. Authors Scott and Stone are wildlife research biologists with the Fish and Wildlife Service's Denver Wildlife Research Center. Scott is stationed in Fort Collins, Colorado. Authors Evans and Patton are principal wildlife biologists with the Forest Service's North Central Forest Experiment Station and Rocky Mountain Forest and Range Experiment Station, respectively. Evans is stationed in Columbia, Missouri, in cooperation with the University of Missouri, while Patton is stationed in Tempe, Arizona, in cooperation with Arizona State University.

Special thanks are due Arthur Singer, who graciously donated the use of his illustrations from "A guide to field identification: Birds of North America," by Robbins, Bruun, and Zim, which are reproduced here with permission of the Western Publishing Company. The distribution maps are also reproduced with the permission of Western Publishing Company. © Copyright 1966 by Western Publishing Company, Inc.

We would like to thank Kimberly Hardin, Beverly Roedner, Mary Gilbert, Steve Blair, and Michael, Leslie, and Mary Stone for their assistance in collecting literature. A special thanks to Jill Whelan for her assistance in literature searches, checking references and scientific names, and assembling this publication. The assistance of Robert Hamre in encouraging and guiding the preparation of this manuscript is acknowledged and very much appreciated.

1
Cavity-Nesting Birds of North American Forests

Many species of cavity-nesting birds have declined because of habitat reduction. In the eastern United States, where primeval forests are gone, purple martins depend almost entirely on man-made nesting structures (Allen and Nice 1952). The hole-nesting population of peregrine falcons disappeared with the felling of the giant trees upon which they depended (Hickey and Anderson 1969). The ivory-billed and red-cockaded woodpeckers are currently on the endangered list, primarily as a result of habitat destruction (Givens 1971, Bent 1939). The wood duck was very scarce in many portions of its range, at least in part, for the same reason and probably owes its present status to provision of nest boxes and protection from overhunting.

Some 85 species of North American birds (table 1) excavate nesting holes, use cavities resulting from decay (natural cavities), or use holes created by other species in dead or deteriorating trees. Such trees, commonly called snags, have often been considered undesirable by forest and recreation managers because they are not esthetically pleasing, conflict with other forest management practices, may harbor forest insect pests, or may be fire or safety hazards. In the past such dead trees were often eliminated from the forest during a timber harvest. As a result, in some areas few nesting sites were left for cavity-nesting birds. Current well-intentioned environmental pressures to emphasize harvesting large dead or dying trees, if realized, would have further adverse effects on such ecologically and esthetically important species as woodpeckers, swallows, wrens, nuthatches, and owls—to name a few.

The majority of cavity-nesting birds are insectivorous. Because they make up a large proportion of the forest-dwelling bird population, they play an important role in the control of forest insect pests (Thomas et al. 1975). Woodpeckers are especially important predators of many species of tree-killing bark beetles (Massey and Wygant 1973). Bruns (1960) summarized the role of birds in the 2 forests:

> Within the community of all animals and plants of the forest, birds form an important factor. The birds generally are not able to break down an insect plague, but their function lies in preventing insect plagues. It is our duty to preserve birds for esthetic as well as economic reasons ... where nesting chances are diminished by forestry work.... It is our duty to further these biological forces [birds, bats, etc.] and to conserve or create a rich and diverse community. By such a prophylactic ... the forests will be better protected than by any other means.

Several of the birds that nest in cavities tend to be resident (non-migrating) species (von Haartman 1968) and thus more amenable to local habitat management practices than migratory species. Nest holes may be limiting for breeding populations of at least some species (von Haartman 1956, Laskey 1940, Troetschler 1976, Kessell 1957). Bird houses have been readily accepted by many natural cavity nesters, and increases in breeding density have resulted from providing such structures (Hamerstrom et al. 1973, Strange et al. 1971, Grenquist 1965), an indication that management of natural snags should be rewarding.

Because nesting requirements vary by bird species, forest type, and geographic location, more research is needed to determine snag species, quality, and density of existing and potential cavity trees that are needed to sustain adequate populations of cavity-nesters. In a Montana study, for example, larch and paper birch snags were most frequently used by cavity-nesters (McClelland and Frissell 1975). The most frequently used trees were large, broken-topped larches (either dead or alive), greater than 25 inches diameter at breast height (dbh), and more than 50 feet tall. No particular snag density was recommended to managers. In the Pacific Northwest, Thomas et al. (1976) suggested about seven snags per acre to maintain 100 percent of the potential maximum breeding populations of cavity-nesters in ponderosa pine forests and six per acre in lodgepole pine and subalpine fir. In Arizona ponderosa pine forests, an average of 2.6 snags per acre (mostly ponderosa) were used by cavity-nesting birds (Scott, in press[1]). The most frequently used snags were trees dead 6 or more years, more than 18 inches dbh, and with more than 40 percent bark cover. The height of the snag was not as important as the diameter, but snags more than 46 feet tall had more holes than did shorter ones. Balda (1975) recommended 2.7 snags per acre to maintain natural bird species diversity and maximum densities in the ponderosa pine forests of Arizona.

3
Important silvical characteristics in the development of nesting cavities include (1) tree size, longevity, and distribution; (2) regeneration by sprouts, and (3) decay in standing trees (Hansen 1966). Although trees less than 14 to 16 inches dbh at maturity are too small to yield cavities appropriate for wood ducks, they may be important for smaller

species. Aspen, balsam fir, bitternut hickory, ironwood, and other trees fall within this range. Short-lived species such as aspen and balsam fir usually form cavities earlier than longer lived trees. Since a major avenue of fungal infection is sprouts, sprouting vigor and the age at which sprouts are produced are important considerations in managing for cavity-producing hardwood trees. Cavity formation in oaks of basal origin is a slow process, but black oak is a good cavity producer as trees approach maturity because although the heartwood decays rapidly the sapwood is resistant (Bellrose et al. 1964). Basswood is a good cavity producer because of its sprouting characteristics. Baumgartner (1939), Gysel (1961), Kilham (1971), Erskine and McLaren (1972), and others presented information on tree cavity formation for wildlife species. More information on the role of decay from branch scars, cutting, and animal damage is needed for different species of trees so that positive management for snags may be encouraged.

Removal of snags is also known to reduce populations of some birds. For example, removal of some live timber and snags in an Arizona ponderosa pine forest reduced cavity-nesting bird populations by 50 percent (Scott[2]). Violet-green swallows, pygmy nuthatches, and northern three-toed woodpeckers accounted for much of the decline. A previously high population of swallows dropped 90 percent, and a low woodpecker population was eliminated. On an adjacent plot, where live trees were harvested but snags were left standing, cavity-nesters increased as they did on a plot where live trees and snags were undisturbed.

Foresters and recreation managers are now more aware of the esthetic and economic values of nongame wildlife, including cavity-nesting birds. In summer of 1977 the U.S. Forest Service established a national snag policy requiring all Regions and Forests to develop guidelines to "provide habitat needed to maintain viable, self-sustaining populations of cavity-nesting and snag-dependent wildlife species." These guidelines are also to include "retention of selected trees, snags, and other flora, to meet future habitat requirements" (USDA Forest Service 1977). 4 Some Forest Service Regions had already established policies for snag management. For example, in 1976 the Arizona-New Mexico Region (USDA Forest Service 1976) recommended that three good quality snags be retained per acre within 500 feet of forest openings and water, with two per acre over the remaining forest. The policy also requires that provisions be made for continued recruitment of future snags; spike-topped trees with cavities and obvious cull trees should be left for future cavity nesters. Some foresters are now using tags to protect the more suitable snags from fuelwood cutters in high-use areas.

In this book, we have summarized both published data and personal observations on the cavity-nesting birds of North America in an attempt to provide land managers with an up-to-date, convenient source of information on the specific requirements of these birds. Bird nomenclature follows the American Ornithologists' Union Checklist of North American Birds (fifth edition, with supplements). Bird illustrations and distribution maps are reprinted with permission of Western Publishing Co. from A Guide to Field Identification of Birds of North America by Robbins et al. (1966). The small range maps indicate where birds are likely to be found during different seasons. Summer or breeding range is identified in red, winter range in blue; purple indicates areas where the species may be found all year. Red cross-hatching identifies areas where migrating birds are likely to be seen only In spring and fall. Length measurements (L) are for birds in their natural position, while W indicates wingspan.

Percentages of the diet under "Food" in species accounts refer to volume, unless otherwise indicated. Since nestlings of most species require insect protein, "Major Foods" refers largely to adult diets. Appendices list common names of plants and animals mentioned in the text, with scientific names when they could be determined.

5
Table 1.—Cavity-nesting birds: tree use and major foods.

Common Name	A	B	C	Page No.	Snag or Tree Use[3] 2	3	4	Major Foods[4] 5	6	7
Black-bellied whistling duck	X			7			X	X		
Wood duck	X	X		8	X	X				X
Common goldeneye	X	X	X	9	X					
Barrow's goldeneye	X	X	X	10	X					
Bufflehead	X	X	X	11	X					X
Hooded merganser	X	X		12		X	X			X
Common merganser	X			13	X	X	X			X
Turkey vulture				14	X	X	X			
Black vulture				15	X	X	X			
Peregrine falcon[5]				16		X	X	X		
Merlin				17	X	X	X	X		X
American kestrel	X			18		X	X	X	X	
Barn owl				19	X	X		X		
Screech owl				20	X	X		X		X
Whiskered owl	X			21		X	X			
Flammulated owl	X			22		X	X			
Hawk owl				23	X	X				X
Pygmy owl				24	X	X		X		X
Ferruginous owl				25		X	X	X		

4

Species	Page						
Elf owl	26	X	X				X
Barred owl	27	X	X		X		
Spotted owl	28	X	X	X	X		X
Boreal owl	29	X	X		X		
Saw-whet owl	30		X	X		X	X
Chimney swift	31		X				X
Vaux's swift	32	X					X X
Coppery-tailed trogon	33		X	X			X X
Common flicker	34	X	X	X			X
Pileated woodpecker	35	X	X	X			X
Red-bellied woodpecker	36	X	X	X			X X
Golden-fronted woodpecker	37		X				X X
Gila woodpecker	38		X				X X
Red-headed woodpecker	39	X	X	X			X X
Acorn woodpecker	40	X	X	X			X X
Lewis' woodpecker	41	X	X				X X X
Yellow-bellied sapsucker	42	X	X	X			X X
Williamson's sapsucker	43	X	X	X			X
Hairy woodpecker	44	X	X	X			X
Downy woodpecker	45	X	X	X			X
Ladder-backed woodpecker	46		X				X X
Nuttall's woodpecker	47		X				X X
Arizona woodpecker	48	X	X	X			X X
Red-cockaded woodpecker	49	X	X	X			X

Species	#				
White-headed woodpecker	50		X		
		X	X		
Black-backed three-toed woodpecker	51		X	X	
		X			
Northern three-toed woodpecker	52		X	X	
		X			
Ivory-billed woodpecker[5]	53	X	X	X	
		X			
Sulphur-bellied flycatcher	54		X		
		X	X		
Great-crested flycatcher	55		X	X	
		X			
Wied's crested flycatcher	56		X		
		X	X		
Ash-throated flycatcher	57		X	X	
		X	X		
Olivaceous flycatcher	58	X	X		
		X			
Western flycatcher	59	X			
		X			
Violet-green swallow	60	X	X		
		X			
Tree swallow	61	X			
		X	X		
Purple martin	62	X	X		
		X			
Black-capped chickadee	63		X		
		X	X		
Carolina chickadee	64	X			
		X	X		
Mexican chickadee	65	X			
		X			
Mountain chickadee	66	X			
		X	X		
Gray-headed chickadee	67		X		
		X			
Boreal chickadee	68	X			
		X	X	X	
Chestnut-backed chickadee	69		X		
		X	X	X	
Tufted titmouse	70	X			
		X	X		
Plain titmouse	71	X			
		X	X		
Bridled titmouse	72	X			
		X			
White-breasted nuthatch	73		X		
		X	X		

Species	#						
Red-breasted nuthatch	74		X				
	X	X					
Brown-headed nuthatch	75		X				
	X		X				
Pygmy nuthatch	76		X				
	X						
Brown creeper	77		X				
	X	X					
House wren	78	X				X	
Brown-throated wren	79		X				
	X	X					
Winter wren	80	X				X	
Bewick's wren	81		X				
	X						
Carolina wren	82		X				
	X						
Eastern bluebird	83		X	X			
	X						
Western bluebird	84		X	X			
	X	X					
Mountain bluebird	85		X	X			
	X	X					
Starling	86	X	X	X		X	
	X	X	X				
Crested myna	87		X				
	X	X	X				
Prothonotary warbler	88		X				
	X	X					
Lucy's warbler	89		X				
	X						
House sparrow	90	X	X	X			
	X	X	X				
European tree sparrow	91		X				
	X	X					

7

Black-bellied whistling duck
Dendrocygna autumnalis
L 13″ W 37″

Habitat: Black-bellied whistling ducks (tree ducks) are found regularly in southern Texas and erratically elsewhere. Open woodlands, groves or thicket borders where ebony, mesquite, retama, huisache, and several species of cacti are dominant in freshwater habitat are preferred (Oberholser 1974, Meanley and Meanley 1958). Range extensions have been facilitated by flooding and impoundments.

Nest: Natural cavities in trees such as live oaks, ebony, willow, mesquite, and hackberry are preferred, but ground nests and nest boxes are sometimes used. The nest can be over land or water, but herbaceous vegetation under "land-bound" nests may be preferred to brush (Bolen et al. 1964). A perch near the cavity entrance may also be a factor in nest tree selection. Open and closed cavities are used. Nest cavities average 8.7 feet above ground or water and 23 inches deep, with 7.0 × 12.5 inch openings (Bellrose 1976). Nesting boxes should be 11 × 11 × 22 inches high at the front and tapered to 20 inches in the rear, with entrances 5 inches in diameter (Bolen 1967). Nest boxes should not be erected unless they are predator proof.

Food: Black-bellied whistling ducks are predominantly grazers (Rylander and Bolen 1974), but they can dabble and dive for aquatic food. Of 92 percent plant materials, sorghum and Bermudagrass predominated, with smartweeds, millets, water stargrass, and corn also occurring in one study (Bolen and Forsyth 1967). In some areas corn and oats are more important in the diet.

8
Wood duck
Aix sponsa
L 13½″   W 28″

Habitat: Wood ducks are associated with bottomland hardwood forests where trees are large enough to provide nesting cavities and where water areas provide food and cover requirements (McGilvrey 1968). Requirements may be met in several important forest types, all of which must be flooded during the early nesting season: (1) southern flood plain, (2) red maple, (3) central flood plain, (4) temporarily flooded oak-hickory, and (5) northern bottomland hardwoods.

Nest: Optimum natural cavities are 20 to 50 feet above the ground with entrance holes of 4 inches in diameter, cavity depths of 2 feet, and cavity bottoms measuring 10 × 10 inches (McGilvrey 1968). Management for cavities more than a half mile from water is not recommended, and dead trees, other than cypress, do not usually contain usable cavities. Good densities of suitable wood-duck cavities have been recorded for many timber types (Bellrose 1976). Nest boxes are readily used by wood ducks, and their use may increase breeding populations, even if natural cavities are abundant, if predators are excluded. Measurements and placement of wood duck boxes have been well described (U.S. Fish and Wildlife Service 1976, Bellrose 1976, McGilvrey 1968).

Food: Wood ducks consume large quantities of acorns, usually in flooded bottoms. Other mast and fleshy fruits also are eaten, as are waste corn and wheat (Bellrose 1976). Smartweed, buttonbush, bulrush, pondweed, cypress, ash, sweet gum, burweed, and arrow arum seeds are used by breeding birds. Skunk cabbage, coontail, and duckweed are also food items. Duckweed is also habitat for invertebrates in the diet (Grice and Rogers 1965).

9
Common goldeneye
Bucephala clangula
L 13″   W 31″

Habitat: The breeding range of the common goldeneye generally coincides with the boreal coniferous forest in North America (Johnsgard 1975, Bellrose 1976). In a Minnesota study, 87 percent of breeding goldeneyes were found on large, sand-bottomed fish lakes (Johnson 1967), while in New Brunswick, this species preferred water areas with marshy shores and adjacent stands of old hardwoods (Carter 1958). In Maine, nests are found in mature hardwoods adjacent to lakes with rocky shores, hard bottoms, and clear water. Shoal waters less than 10 feet deep with an irregular shoreline provide brood shelter and protective vegetation necessary for duckling food (Gibbs 1961).

Nest: Common goldeneyes used and were more successful in open top or "bucket" cavities than in enclosed cavities in New Brunswick (Prince 1968). Most nests were in silver maples on wetter sites or American elms on drier sites and aspen in northern conifer forests. Nest trees averaged 23 inches in diameter with cavity dimensions of 8 inches in diameter and 18 inches deep; most entrances were 6 to 40 feet above ground (Prince 1968). Wooden nest boxes measuring 12 × 12 × 24 inches with elliptical entrances 3½ × 4½ inches were used extensively in Minnesota (Johnson 1967).

Food: Of 395 stomachs examined by Cottam (1939), crustaceans (32 percent), insects (28 percent), and molluscs (10 percent) were primary animal foods (total, 73.9 percent). Crabs, crayfish, amphipods, caddisfly larvae, water boatmen, naiads of dragonflies, damselflies, and mayflies were also found. Pondweed, wild celery, and seeds of pondweed and bulrushes were important plant materials.

10
Barrow's goldeneye
Bucephala islandica
L 13″ W 31″

Habitat: Barrow's goldeneyes attain their highest breeding population levels in western North America on moderately alkaline lakes of small to medium size in parkland areas. Open water is a necessity throughout the range, but frequently goldeneyes favor a dense growth of submerged aquatics such as sago pondweed and widgeon grass. The abundance of aquatic invertebrates may be more important than nesting cavities in determining distribution (Johnsgard 1975).

Nest: This species is not an obligate tree nester, and has been reported to use holes in banks or lava beds, rock crevices, ground under shrubs and on islands, haylofts, crows' nests, and the outer walls of peat shelters for sheep in Iceland (Harris et al. 1954). However, the usual site is in dead stubs or trees such as aspen, Douglas-fir, and ponderosa pine within 100 feet of water (Palmer 1976). Deserted pileated woodpecker or common flicker cavities enlarged by natural decay are readily used (Palmer 1976). Cavity entrances from 3.0 to 3.9 inches in diameter, cavity depths between 9.8 and 52.9 inches, and cavity diameters between 6.5 and 9.0 inches have been reported (Johnsgard 1975). Nest boxes have been used around high lakes in the Cascade Mountains (Bellrose 1976).

Food: Food of 71 adult Barrow's goldeneyes consisted of 36 percent insects, 19 percent molluscs, 18 percent crustaceans, 4 percent other animals, and 22 percent plants (Cottom 1939). Naiads of dragonflies and damselflies, caddisfly and midge larvae, blue mussels, amphipods, isopods, and crayfish were important animal foods, and pondweeds and wild celery were primary plant foods.

11
Bufflehead
Bucephala albeola
L 10″ W 24″

Habitat: Buffleheads favor small ponds and lakes in open woodlands (Godfrey 1966). In British Columbia, most nesting is in the interior Douglas-fir zone while poplar communities are usually used in Alberta, and ponderosa pine types are preferred in California. Scattered breeding records in Oregon, Wyoming, and Idaho are primarily in subalpine lodgepole pine, and in Alaska (Erskine 1971) Engelmann spruce and cottonwood stands are used for nesting.

Nest: Of 204 nests observed from California to Alaska, 107 were in aspen trees, 44 in Douglas-fir, 14 in balsam poplar and black cottonwood, 12 in ponderosa pine, 11 in poplar, and 16 in a few other coniferous and deciduous trees (Palmer 1976). Buffleheads prefer unaltered flicker holes in aspen. Dead trees close to (within 220 yards) or in water are preferred, and "bucket" or open top cavities are rarely used (Erskine 1971). Forestry practices that leave stubs near water while clearing away most ground litter and slash that might hinder ducklings from reaching water are to be encouraged. Nest boxes used by captive buffleheads had entrances 2⅞ inches wide with cavities 7 inches in diameter and 16 inches deep (Johnsgard 1975).

Food: Buffleheads consume mostly animal material. Insects make up 70 percent of summer foods in freshwater habitat. Midge, mayfly, and caddisfly larvae, and naiads of dragonflies and damselflies are also consumed. Water boatmen are the most widely distributed, important food. Plant food was found in many stomachs but much was fiber and was probably taken while catching aquatic insects. Pondweed and bulrush seeds were frequently consumed plant items. Dragonfly and damselfly larvae are important in the diet of ducklings in all areas (Erskine 1971).

12
Hooded merganser
Lophodytes cucullatus
L 13″ W 26″

Habitat: Although hooded mergansers prefer wooded, clear water streams, they also use the wooded shorelines of lakes. Drainage of swamps and river bottoms, removal of snags, and other human activities have been detrimental to this species as they have been to wood ducks. Hooded mergansers are more easily disturbed by man and far more sensitive to a decline in water quality than are wood ducks. Breeding densities often seem more related to food abundance and availability than to nesting cavities (Johnsgard 1975).

Nest: Cavities at any height may be selected in any species of tree; the size and shape of the cavity are apparently not important (Bent 1923). Natural cavities chosen are similar to those used by wood ducks but with smaller optimum dimensions. Frequent use of nest boxes has been reported in Missouri, Mississippi, and Oregon (Bellrose 1976). In Oregon, boxes were placed 30 to 50 feet apart in sets of 8 (Morse et al. 1969). Some of the most southerly nesting records of this species are from wood duck nest boxes (Bellrose 1976).

Food: The food habits of hooded mergansers are not well known, but are apparently more diversified than those of common mergansers. Of 138 stomachs taken from various locations in the United States, rough fishes made up 24.5 percent, game fish and unidentified fish fragments 19.4 percent, crayfish 22.3 percent, other crustaceans 10.3 percent, and aquatic and other insects 13.4 percent (Palmer 1976). Acorns are sometimes eaten in large quantities. Frogs, tadpoles, and molluscs such as snails are also consumed.

13
Common merganser
Mergus merganser
L 18″ W 37″

Habitat: Common mergansers prefer cool, clear waters of northern boreal or western forests, although at times they have nested as far south as North Carolina and Mexico. Ponds associated with the upper portions of rivers in northern forested regions are often used (Johnsgard 1975). As with hooded mergansers, clear water is needed for foraging.

Nest: Although hollow trees are the usual location, ground nests under thick cover or in rock crevices are not uncommon. A wide variety of other locations have been reported such as chimneys, hawk nests, bridge supports, and old buildings. The species of tree used for nesting and the height of the cavity are apparently unimportant (Foreman 1976). Nest sites are usually close to water (Bellrose 1976) and are used repeatedly, probably by the same female (Palmer 1976). Artificial nest boxes have been accepted, especially in Europe. Preferred dimensions are 9.1 to 11 inches wide, and 33.5 to 39.4 inches high, with 4.7×4.7-inch entrances, 19.7 to 23.6 inches above the base of the nest box (Johnsgard 1975).

Food: Programs to reduce populations of this fish-eating merganser have increased trout and salmon production in several areas, at least temporarily. Generally, common mergansers are opportunistic feeders with salmon taken extensively in some areas and suckers, chubs, and eels in others. In warm-water areas, food is usually rough and forage fish such as carp, suckers, gizzard shad, perch, and catfish. In some areas, water plants, salamanders, insects, or molluscs may be important in the diet of this species (Palmer 1976).

14
Turkey vulture
Cathartes aura
L 25″ W 72″

Habitat: Turkey vultures soar over most of the forest types of the United States and southern Canada, with the exception of the pine and spruce-fir stands in the extreme northeastern United States. In search of food this common carrion eater makes use of the forest openings created by roads, powerline rights-of-way, clearcuts, and abandoned fields.

Nest: Preferred nest sites are often at a premium because of the bird's large size and the shortage of large snags. The smell of carrion around the nest necessitates a well-protected site to lessen predator losses. The nest site is almost always at or near ground level (Bent 1937). Although nesting sites are commonly located in hollow trees or hollow logs lying on the ground, these vultures will nest on cliffs, in caves, and in dense shrubbery (Gingrich 1914, Townsend 1914). These birds will return to the same nesting site year after year unless the site has been severely disturbed (Jackson 1903, Kempton 1927).

Food: Turkey vultures are scavengers and carrion-eaters, often hunting along roads where animals have been struck by automobiles. They feed on snakes, toads, rats, mice, and other available animal matter. Often a dozen or more vultures will gather at and feed on a large carcass.

15
Black vulture
Coragyps atratus
L 22″ W 54″

Habitat: The black vulture is found in the southern Great Plains, southeastern pine forests, oak-hickory forests, and intermediate oak-pine forests. It is a more southern species than the turkey vulture.

Nest: Like turkey vultures, black vultures nest under a wide variety of conditions. They use the nest site as found without adding nesting materials (Hoxie 1886, Bent 1937). Hollow stumps or standing trees are favorite nesting sites when they are available; otherwise, eggs are laid on the ground, often in dense thickets of palmetto, yucca, or tall sawgrass (Bent 1937). Nests have been reported in abandoned buildings.

Food: This carrion-eater is often found in towns and cities, feeding on animal wastes, scraps, or garbage. Forests are used primarily for roosting and nesting sites, whereas feeding is usually in more open areas and along highways, where animal carcasses are more plentiful.

16
Peregrine falcon
Falco peregrinus
L 15″ W 40″

Habitat: The peregrine falcon is found in tundra regions, northern boreal forests, lodgepole pine and subalpine fir, spruce-fir, southern hardwood-conifer, cold desert shrubs, and prairies—mainly in open country and along streams. It is also found around salt and freshwater marshes (Fyfe 1969, Hickey and Anderson 1969, Nelson 1969). This species is currently classified as "Endangered" in the United States.

Nest: Although the peregrine falcon is currently considered a cliff-nester, records indicate that it once nested in tree cavities (Goss 1878, Ridgway 1889, Ganier 1932, Bellrose 1938, Spofford 1942, 1943, 1945, 1947, Peterson 1948). The peregrine still uses cavities in broken-off trunks in Europe (Hickey 1942), but the hole-nesting population of America apparently disappeared with the felling of the great trees on which they depended (Hickey and Anderson 1969).

Food: The peregrine falcon feeds primarily on birds ranging in size from mallards to warblers, which are usually stunned or killed in flight. Mammals and large insects form only an insignificant portion of the diet (Bent 1938). White and Roseneau (1970) found remains of fish in the stomachs of peregrines in Alaska, and suggested that fish may be more common in some peregrine diets than the literature indicates.

17
Merlin
Falco columbarius
L 12″ W 23″

Habitat: The merlin is usually found in open stands of boreal forest, Douglas-fir—sitka spruce, poplar-aspen-birch-willow, ponderosa pine—Douglas-fir, oak woodlands, and saltwater marshes (Craighead and Craighead 1940, Lawrence 1949, Brown and Weston 1961).

Nest: Like the peregrine falcon, most cavity nests for the merlin were reported before 1910, when it was nesting in cavities of poplars, cottonwoods, and American linden trees (Bendire 1892, Houseman 1894, Dippie 1895). The merlin usually uses tree nests built by other large birds (such as hawks, crows, and magpies) but sometimes nests on the ground under bushes or on cliffs and cutbanks.

Food: Brown and Amadon (1968) found that birds made up 80 percent (by weight) of the food for merlins, insects 15 percent, and mammals 5 percent. Ferguson (1922) examined 298 stomachs and found 4 mammals, 318 birds, and 967 insects. Birds found in the stomachs included small shorebirds, small game birds, and songbirds (which are normally captured in flight). Insect prey consisted of crickets, grasshoppers, dragonflies, beetles, and caterpillars (Bent 1938), while mammals included pocket gophers, squirrels, mice, and bats (Fisher 1893).

18
American kestrel
Falco sparverius
L 8½″ W 21″

Habitat: The American kestrel is the smallest and most common falcon in North America, occurring in open and semi-open country throughout the continent. In the Rocky Mountain region, kestrels are most abundant on the plains, but do nest up to 8,000 feet elevation in the Douglas-fir, ponderosa pine, and pinyon-juniper forest types (Scott and Patton 1975, Bailey and Niedrach 1965). They have been observed on the highest peaks after the nesting season (Bailey and Niedrach 1965).

Nest: Nest sites vary greatly, but kestrels prefer natural cavities or old woodpecker holes. The following nest sites are reported in order of usage: common flicker holes, natural cavities, cavities in arroyo banks or cliffs, buildings, magpie nests, and man-made nesting boxes (Bailey and Niedrach 1965, Bent 1938, Roest 1957, Forbush and May 1939). Nest boxes, approximately 10 × 10 × 15 inches, should be located 10 to 35 feet above ground with a 3-inch entrance hole. Natural cavities or nest boxes should be available along edges of forest openings (Bailey and Niedrach 1965, Hamerstrom et al. 1973, Pearson 1936).

Food: Kestrels hunt from high exposed perches overlooking forest openings, fields, or pastures. Food consists primarily of insects (often grasshoppers), small mammals, and an occasional bird (Bent 1938).

19
Barn owl
Tyto alba
L 14″   W 44″

Habitat: The barn owl inhabits most of the forest types in the United States except the higher elevation types in the Rocky Mountains. They are usually considered uncommon residents because their silent nocturnal habits render them undetectable by most casual observers. Barn owls are also birds of the open country, and adapt readily to areas occupied by man (Marti 1974).

Nest: Before the coming of man, barn owls nested in natural cavities in trees, cliffs, or arroyo walls, but now they also nest in barns, church steeples, bird boxes, mine shafts, and dovecotes (Bailey and Niedrach 1965, Reed 1897).

Food: Barn owls frequent areas where small mammals are plentiful; mice, voles, rats, gophers, and ground squirrels are major food items. Birds other than those such as house sparrows and blackbirds, which have communal roosts, are only rarely taken (Marti 1974).

20
Screech owl
Otus asio
L 8″   W 22″

Habitat: This small owl is found in most forest types below 8,000 feet elevation throughout the United States. Screech owls prefer widely spaced trees, interspersed with grassy open spaces, for hunting. Meadow edges and fruit orchards are favored throughout the eastern United States.

Nest: Like other owls, the male screech owl defends a nesting and feeding territory. Maples, apples, and sycamores with natural cavities or pines with woodpecker holes are preferred in the East (Bent 1938). Along the drainage systems of the plains areas, natural cavities or common flicker holes in cottonwood trees are preferred (Bailey and Niedrach 1965). Nest boxes in orchards or residential areas are often used. Hamerstrom (1972) recommended a nesting box 8 × 8 × 8 inches with a 3-inch entrance hole.

Food: Screech owls are among the most nocturnal owls and are rarely seen feeding. Major food items are mice and insects. Fisher (1893) examined 255 stomachs of screech owls and found birds in 15 percent of them, mice in 36 percent, and insects in 39 percent.

Korschgen and Stuart (1972) found mostly small mammals in 419 screech owl pellets from western Missouri. The volume of the screech owl pellets was predominantly meadow mice, white-footed mice, and cotton rats.

21
Whiskered owl
Otus trichopsis
L 6½"   W 16"

Habitat: The small whiskered owl is generally found in the dense oak or oak-pine forests of southern Arizona, southwestern New Mexico, and into Mexico.

Nest: Nests have been reported in both natural cavities and old woodpecker holes located in oak, cottonwood, willow, walnut, sycamore, and juniper trees (Bent 1938). Karalus and Eckert (1974) suggest that white oak is one of the favorite nest sites, and that these small owls prefer to nest in cavities in the limbs of trees rather than in the trunk.

Food: Black crickets, hairy crickets, moths, grasshoppers, large beetle larvae, and centipedes are the principal elements of the diet (Jacot 1931). In addition to those mentioned by Jacot, Karalus and Eckert (1974) list praying mantids, roaches, cicadas, scorpions, and small mammals as part of the diet.

22
Flammulated owl
Otus flammeolus
L 6"   W 14"

Habitat: The flammulated owl normally is not found in cutover forests or in pure stands of conifers but requires some understory or intermixture of oaks in the forest (Phillips et al. 1964). It occurs in ponderosa pine, spruce-fir, lodgepole pine, aspen, and pinyon-juniper forest types (Grinnell and Miller 1944, Karalus and Eckert 1974).

Nest: Nests are usually located in abandoned flicker or other woodpecker holes, but flammulated owls may take over occupied nests (Karalus and Eckert 1974). Their nests have been reported in pine, oak, and aspen snags (Bent 1938).

Food: The flammulated owl is almost entirely insectivorous, but it occasionally captures small mammals and birds. In the few stomachs that have been examined, items reported were various beetles, moths, grasshoppers, crickets, caterpillars, ants, other insects, spiders, and scorpions (Bent 1938). Kenyon (1947) examined the stomach contents of one owl and found 4 crane flies, 1 caddisfly, 7 moths, 11 harvestman spiders, and 1 long-horned grasshopper; the bird had apparently choked to death on the grasshopper.

23
Hawk owl
Surnia ulula
L 14"   W 33"

Habitat: The hawk owl inhabits much of the northern poplar, spruce, pine, birch, tamarac, and willow forests where such forests are broken by small prairie burns and bogs (Henderson 1919).

Nest: Hawk owls usually nest in natural cavities or in enlarged holes of pileated woodpeckers and flickers. Nests have been reported in birch, spruce, tamarac, poplar snags (Henderson 1919, 1925, Bent 1938), and occasionally on cliffs or in crow's nests.

Food: This owl hunts extensively during the day and feeds on small mammals, birds, and insects (Bent 1938). Mendall (1944) examined 21 hawk owl stomachs; all contained meadow or red-backed mice; two owls had also fed on shrews.

24
Pygmy owl
Glaucidium gnoma
L 6″ W 15″

Habitat: The pygmy owl is found in most of the western wooded areas from western Canada into Mexico. It is probably most abundant in open coniferous or mixed forests and is reported specifically in ponderosa pine, mixed conifer, and fir-redwood-cedar forests.

Nest: This owl usually nests in old woodpecker holes ranging in size from those constructed by hairy woodpeckers up to and including those of the flickers from 8 to 75 feet above ground (Bent 1938).

Food: Mice and large insects are probably the most common prey of the pygmy owl, although other small mammals, birds, amphibians, and reptiles have been reported (Bent 1938). Brock (1958) found one vole, a deer mouse, and a Jerusalem cricket in the stomach of one bird and reported seeing another pygmy owl take a Nuttall's woodpecker. We observed one pygmy owl in Arizona carrying a small vole. They have also been observed taking mice in the mountains west of Denver, and taking birds in the vicinity of feeders in Boulder, Colorado (Richard Pillmore pers. comm.[6]).

25
Ferruginous owl
Glaucidium brasilianum
L 6″ W 15″

Habitat: This uncommon small owl inhabits the saguaro cactus in Sonoran deserts and wooded river bottoms near the Mexican border.

Nest: Nests are in abandoned woodpecker holes in mesquite, cottonwood, and saguaro cactus. Nest heights range from 10 to 40 feet above ground (Bent 1938, Karalus and Eckert 1974).

Food: The diet of the ferruginous owl consists primarily of small birds; however, insects, small mammals, invertebrates, reptiles, and amphibians are occasionally eaten (Karalus and Eckert 1974).

26
Elf owl
Micrathene whitneyi
L 5¼″ W 15″

Habitat: The elf owl is restricted to the southwestern United States where it is found primarily in the saguaro cactus deserts, bottomland sycamore and cottonwood stands and in conifer-hardwood forests at high elevations.

Nest: One of the most common nest sites of the elf owl is in old woodpecker holes in saguaro cactus. It has also been reported nesting in cavities in sycamore, walnut, mesquite, and pine trees (Ligon 1967, Bent 1938, Hayes and James 1963). Cavities are usually located in snags or in dead branches of living trees.

Food: Elf owls feed almost entirely on insects, particularly beetles, moths, and crickets. They also feed on centipedes and scorpions and have been reported to take an occasional reptile (Ligon 1967).

27
Barred owl
Strix varia
L 17″ W 44″

Habitat: Barred owls are common in southern swamps and moist river bottoms of the Midwest, and less common but widespread in northern forests. These owls are found in all of the eastern forest types. Although they use white pine, these large owls prefer oak woods and mixed hardwood-conifer stands (Nicholls and Warner 1972). Preferred oak woods contain dead and dying trees for cavities and are free of dense understory, thus facilitating unobstructed flying and attacking of prey.

Nest: Natural cavities in hollow trees are preferred by barred owls. If these are unavailable, deserted crow, raptor, or squirrel nests are occasionally used (Pearson 1936, Bent 1938). Hollow trees used usually have hunting perches with good views. Recommended nest box size is 13 × 15 × 16 inches deep, with an entrance hole 8 inches in diameter (Hamerstrom 1972). Nest boxes will have a better chance of being used if they are placed near woods and streams.

Food: Barred owls are nocturnal hunters. More than half of the food items taken in western Missouri consisted of meadow mice, cottontail rabbits, and cotton rats (Korschgen and Stuart 1972).

28
Spotted owl
Strix occidentalis
L 16″ W 42″

Habitat: This uncommon owl occurs in most old-age conifer associations in the western United States. Forsman (1976) located 123 pairs in Oregon, and 95 percent occupied undisturbed old-growth conifer forests. Karalus and Eckert (1974) described the habitat as being dense fir forests, heavily wooded cliffsides, narrow canyons, and sometimes stream valleys well stocked with oak, sycamore, willow, cottonwood, and alder.

Nest: Forsman (1976) found spotted owls nesting in the holes of living old-growth conifers, particularly Douglas-fir. Nest trees typically had secondary crowns and broken tops caused by parasite infection. Cavities were located inside the tops of hollow trunks 62 to 180 feet above ground. Dunn (1901) reported spotted owls nesting in cavities in live and dead oak and sycamore trees. Spotted owls also nest in cavities in cliffs, and occasionally in abandoned nests of other large birds (Bent 1938).

Food: The major food items of the spotted owl are mammals and birds, with occasional insects and amphibians. Forsman (1976) found that mammals made up 90 percent of the total biomass taken; the major prey species were flying squirrels and wood rats. Marshall (1942) examined 23 pellets and stomach contents of 5 spotted owls and found 6 bats, 4 mice, 31 crickets, 12 flying squirrels, 1 mole, 1 shrew, 4 songbirds, 2 smaller owls, and 1 amphibian.

29
Boreal owl
Aegolius funereus
L 10″ W 24″

Habitat: This northern owl is normally found in the mixed conifer-hardwood forests of Canada (Peterson 1961). One juvenile reported in Colorado during August suggests that this owl may nest in the southern Rocky Mountains (Bailey and Niedrach 1965). Boreal owls are confined to evergreen woods and dense alder, white pine, and spruce forests.

Nest: Old flicker and pileated woodpecker holes are preferred, usually at a height of 10 to 25 feet (Fisher 1893, Preble 1908, Tufts 1925, Lawrence 1932). Conifer snags seems to be preferred for nest trees, although hardwoods have been used (Bent 1938).

Food: The main portion of the boreal owl's diet consists of small rodents. Mendall (1944) examined the contents of 20 stomachs in Maine and found 73 percent mice (chiefly meadow voles) and 20 percent short-tailed shrews. Pigeons and grasshoppers made up the remaining 7 percent. In Ontario, Catling (1972) found 86.2 percent meadow voles, 5.6 percent deer mice, 4.2 percent star-nosed moles, 2.7 percent masked shrews, and 1.4 percent short-tailed shrews. Small birds, bats, insects, amphibians, and reptiles are also occasionally eaten (Karalus and Eckert 1974).

30
Saw-whet owl
Aegolius acadicus
L 7″ W 17″

Habitat: Saw-whet owls are small, nocturnal hunters of the deep north woods. They nest in the Rocky Mountains up to about 11,000 feet (Bailey and Niedrach 1965). This widely distributed owl nests in most of the forest types throughout the northern half of the United States, but only rarely do they nest as far south as central Missouri.

Nest: These small owls prefer to nest in old flicker or other woodpecker holes (Bent 1938). Nesting habitat may be improving in areas where Dutch Elm disease has infested many elms, and woodpeckers have drilled nest holes (Hamerstrom 1972). Saw-whets will use nesting boxes if sawdust or straw is provided. Nest boxes should be 6 × 6 × 9 inches with a 2.5-inch entrance hole (Hamerstrom 1972).

Food: Saw-whet owls consume mostly small mammals and insects. Specific food items include mice, shrews, young squirrels, chipmunks, bats, beetles, grasshoppers, and occasionally small birds (Scott and Patton 1975, Burton 1973, Hamerstrom 1972, Bent 1938).

31
Chimney swift
Chaetura pelagica
L 5" W 12½"

Habitat: Chimney swifts are found throughout the eastern half of the United States in wooded and open areas. They have adopted to man-made structures and are no longer dependent upon hollow trees for nesting and roosting.

Nest: Originally chimney swifts nested in hollow trees, especially sycamores. They now use chimneys, barn silos, cisterns, and wells (Pearson 1936). Their nests are made of twigs, which are glued to a vertical surface with saliva to form a "half-saucer" (Forbush and May 1939).

Food: Chimney swifts feed almost entirely on flying insects but will sometimes take small caterpillars hanging from tree branches or leaves (Forbush and May 1939).

32
Vaux's swift
Chaetura vauxi
L 4½"

Habitat: This small swift is most likely to be found in river valleys among dense Douglas-fir and redwood forests in the western United States.

Nest: Nests are usually located in tall hollow snags in burned or logged areas and are made from twigs (Peterson 1961, Robbins et al. 1966). Nests have been reported in unused chimneys and under building eaves (Bent 1940).

Food. Flying insects such as mosquitoes, gnats, flies, and small beetles captured in flight probably make up the entire diet (Bent 1940).

33
Coppery-tailed trogon
Trogon elegans

L 10″

Habitat: Coppery-tailed trogons can be found along riparian streams and in pine-oak forests in Arizona, southwestern New Mexico, and southern Texas.

Nest: Nests are found 12 to 40 feet above the ground in deserted large woodpecker holes (Bent 1940). Cottonwood and sycamore snags are usually selected for nests. Of the 34 species in the family Trogonidae, this is the only one that breeds in the United States (Wetmore 1964).

Food: There is little information on the food of these birds, but apparently both animal and vegetable matter are included in the diet. Bent (1940) reported on stomach contents of two birds. One contained adult and larvae of moths and butterflies; the other contained 68 percent insects and 32 percent fruits. Insect food included grasshoppers, praying mantids, stink bugs, leaf beetles, and larvae of hawk moth, sawfly, and miscellaneous other insects. Vegetable food consisted of fruits of cissus and red pepper and undetermined plant fiber.

34
Common flicker
Colaptes auratus
L 10½″

Habitat: Flickers are commonly found near large trees in open woodlands, fields, and meadows throughout North America. In winter, they occasionally seek shelter in coniferous woods or swamps. Previously three species were recognized: the yellow-shafted of the East, the red-shafted of the West, and the gilded of the southwestern desert. These are now considered a single species.

Nest: Flickers prefer to nest in open country or in lightly wooded suburban areas where park-like situations are plentiful (Bent 1939). Conner et al. (1975) reported that flickers usually nest in edge habitats and, in extensive forested areas, nest only in or around openings. Flickers excavate nest holes with a 2.75-inch entrance hole diameter in dead trees or dead limbs of many species of trees including aspen, cottonwood, oak, willow, sycamore, pine, and juniper. Nests are sometimes as high as 100 feet but usually between 10 and 30 feet (Scott and Patton 1975, Lawrence 1967).

Food: Sixty percent of common flicker food is animal matter. Of this, 75 percent is ants, more than taken by any other North American bird. Some flicker stomachs have contained over 2,000 ants. The rest of the insect material includes beetles, wasps, caterpillars, grubs, and crickets. The vegetable portion of the diet includes weed seeds, cultivated grain, and the fruit of wild shrubs and trees (Bent 1939, Forbush and May 1939).

35
Pileated Woodpecker
Dryocopus pileatus
L 15″

Habitat: Forests of heavy timber and secondary growth consisting of mixed deciduous and coniferous trees are the preferred year-round habitat for pileated woodpeckers. These large woodpeckers have become less abundant over much of their former range where extensive agriculture or logging practices have eliminated large tracts of old growth forests. In the Ozarks, they are plentiful wherever extensive forests remain, preferring areas where past cutting practices (early 1900's) have left scattered large cull trees throughout.

Nest: Pileated woodpecker nests have been found in beech, poplar, tulip-popular, birch, oak, hickory, maple, hemlock, pine, ash, elm, basswood, and aspen trees. Cavity heights range from 15 to 70 feet, with an entrance hole up to 4 inches in diameter (Hoyt 1941, 1957). Tall dead trees with smooth surfaces and few limbs are preferred. One tree may be used for several years, but rarely is a nest hole reused. This behavior provides cavities for other wildlife, including wood ducks, owls, and squirrels (Hoyt 1957). Timber stands with sawtimber of 15 to 18 inches dbh provide adequate habitat if there is a supply of dead and decaying trees (Conner et al. 1975).

Food: Insects make up more than 70 percent of the food of pileated woodpeckers. Ants (especially carpenter ants) and beetles are the major food items. In the fall, dogwood berries, wild cherries, acorns, and other wild fruit are included in the diet (Bent 1939).

36
Red-bellied woodpecker
Melanerpes carolinus
L 8½"

Habitat: Red-bellied woodpeckers are common throughout southeastern forest types. This bird has habits similar to those of the red-headed woodpecker, except that the red-headed prefers open woodlands, farm yards, and field edges whereas the red-bellied prefers larger expanses of forest. Bailey and Niedrach (1965) reported that the red-bellied woodpecker is extending its range westward up the river valleys of the Great Plains.

Nest: These woodpeckers most commonly excavate nest holes in dead limbs of living trees. Excavations were found in a wide variety of tree species, and ranged from 33 to 72 feet above ground (Reller 1972). Cavities are usually located in mature timber stands. Between September and January, males and females roost in separate holes. Often one of the roost holes (usually that of the female) becomes the nest site (Kilham 1958).

Food: Although primarily insectivorous, red-bellied woodpeckers consume more vegetable matter than most woodpeckers. Insects that are eaten include ants, adult and larval beetles, and caterpillars. Vegetation eaten includes grain, berries, and fruits of holly, dogwood, and poison ivy. Acorns and berries are stored in crevices in the fall (Kilham 1963, Bent 1939).

37
Golden-fronted woodpecker
Melanerpes aurifrons
L 8½"

Habitat: The golden-fronted woodpecker's preferred habitat is mesquite and riparian woodlands in Texas and Oklahoma. Cooke (1888) listed this species as an abundant resident of the lower Rio Grande Valley, Texas, in 1884.

Nest: Nesting behavior of the golden-fronted is similar to that of the red-bellied woodpecker (Pearson 1936). Tall trees of pecan, oak, and mesquite are the major species used for nesting (Bent 1939). Occasionally fence posts, telephone poles, and bird boxes are used (Reed 1965).

Food: The diet of the golden-fronted woodpecker consists of both insects and vegetable matter. Grasshoppers make up more than half of the animal matter and other insects include beetles and ants (Pearson 1936, Bent 1939). Vegetable matter consumed consists of corn, acorns, wild fruits, and berries (Bent 1939).

38
Gila woodpecker
Melanerpes uropygialis
L 8¼"

Habitat: This woodpecker is found on desert mesas in association with creosote bush, mesquite, and saguaro cactus from central Arizona to edges of adjacent states. It is also common in river bottoms and in foothill canyons among cottonwoods, willows, and sycamores.

Nest: The Gila woodpecker excavates holes in saguaro cacti for nests. Cottonwoods, willows, and mesquites are also used at higher elevations (Bent 1939, Ligon 1961).

Food: The diet of the Gila woodpecker consists of ants, beetles, grasshoppers, fruits from saguaro cactus, and mistletoe berries (Bent 1939). This woodpecker has been reported to remove eggs from the nests of various songbirds.

39
Red-headed woodpecker
Melanerpes erythrocephalus
L 7½"

Habitat: Red-headed woodpeckers prefer to nest and roost in open areas. Farmyards, field edges, and timber stands that have been treated with herbicides or burned are preferred habitats. Redheads are attracted to areas with many dead snags and lush herbaceous ground cover, but not to woods with closed canopies. They are found throughout the East and along wooded streams of the prairie to eastern Colorado and Wyoming. Competition for nesting space is often intensive where starlings are abundant (Bailey and Niedrach 1965).

Nest: Red-headed woodpeckers most commonly excavate holes in the trunks of dead trees. Holes are excavated from 24 to 65 feet above the ground and the 1.8-inch diameter entrance hole often faces south or west (Reller 1972). These woodpeckers may excavate new holes each year, or use old nest sites.

Food: Red-headed woodpeckers consume about half animal matter (mostly insects) and half vegetable matter. Occasionally the eggs or the young of other birds are destroyed. Although a wide variety of vegetable matter is consumed, acorns from pin oak comprise a large portion of the winter diet. Nuts are stored whole or in pieces in cracks and crevices in bark, and in cavities which are sealed with bits of bark when full. These birds also store insects (especially grasshoppers) along with acorns in cavities and crevices (Kilham 1963, Bent 1939).

40
Acorn woodpecker
Melanerpes formicivorus
L 8″

Habitat: The acorn woodpecker is a common resident of mixed oak-pine woodland and adjacent open grassland from Oregon along the Pacific Coast to the southwestern United States.

Nest: Acorn woodpeckers are communal nesters, and the young are fed by the entire group (Wetmore 1964). They usually excavate holes in ponderosa pine, but live and dead oaks of various species, sycamore, cottonwood, and willow are also used for nests. Their old holes are important for secondary cavity nesters such as small owls, purple martins, violet-green swallows, nuthatches, house wrens, and kestrels (Bent 1939).

Food: As the name implies, acorn woodpeckers feed mostly on acorns which are stored in holes drilled in communal trees. Sap from several species of oaks also is consumed from midwinter to summer (MacRoberts and MacRoberts 1972). About 25 percent of the diet is insects, including grasshoppers, ants, beetles, and flies (Bent 1939). Almonds, walnuts, and pecans are eaten when they are available.

41
Lewis' woodpecker
Melanerpes lewis
L 9″

Habitat: Open or parklike ponderosa pine forest is probably the major breeding habitat of the Lewis' woodpecker. These woodpeckers also nest in burned over stands of Douglas-fir, mixed conifer, pinyon-juniper, riparian, and oak woodlands (Bock 1970).

Nest: The Lewis' woodpecker generally excavates its own nest cavity, but will use natural cavities or holes excavated in previous years. Bock (1970) summarized the following nest data: height range 5 to 170 feet; 47 nests in dead stubs and 17 in live trees; 29 nests in conifers, 31 in cottonwood and sycamore, 6 in oaks, 2 in power poles, 1 in juniper, and 1 in catalpa. At Boca Reservoir, California, 10 of 11 nests were in dead ponderosa pines, and the other was in a hollow section of a living pine.

Food: Insects, including flies, ladybird beetle larvae, tent caterpillars, ants, and mayflies, were the primary food of Lewis' woodpeckers during spring and summer (Bock 1970). Fruits and berries were the most frequently used food in late summer and fall, while winter food consisted mostly of acorns and almonds gathered and stored in crevices of dead trees, power poles, and oak bark. Hadow (1973) reported that, on snowy days when insects were inactive, Lewis' woodpeckers in southeastern Colorado spent 99 percent of their feeding time feeding from caches of acorns and corn kernels.

42
Yellow-bellied sapsucker
Sphyrapicus varius
L 7¾"

Habitat: The yellow-bellied sapsucker (sometimes called red-naped) is most abundant along streams in mixed hardwood-conifer forests. It is also found in ponderosa pine, aspen, mixed conifer, lodgepole pine, and in mixed stands of fir-larch-pine.

Nest: Yellow-bellied sapsuckers usually nest in cavities in snags or live trees with rotten heartwood. Aspen seems to be the preferred species (Howell 1952, Lawrence 1967, Kilham 1971), but nests have also been found in ponderosa pine, birch, elm, butternut, cottonwood, alder, willow, beech, maple, and fir (Bent 1939). Kilham (1971) noted that nest trees were often infected by the Fomes fungus. Nest height varies from 5 to 70 feet above ground. The same nest tree is often used repeatedly, but a new cavity is excavated each year.

Food: Sap is eaten throughout the year by the yellow-bellied sapsucker, but the amount taken and tree species used vary seasonally (Tate 1973, Lawrence 1967). The birds regularly tap one or two "favorite trees" in their area; Oliver (1970) found that these tend to be trees which have been wounded (by logging, porcupines, etc.). About 80 percent of the insect food taken consists of ants (McAtee 1911). Other insects in their diet include beetles and wasps, but none of the woodboring larvae. The fruits of dogwood, black alder, Virginia creeper, and blackberries are included in the small portion of vegetable matter eaten (Bent 1939).

43
Williamson's sapsucker
Sphyrapicus thyroideus
L 8¼"

Habitat: This sapsucker prefers mixed conifer-hardwood forests of the Rocky Mountain region but also inhabits the subalpine spruce-fir-lodgepole zone, and ponderosa pine, Douglas-fir, and aspen forests.

Nest: The choice of tree species for nesting seems to differ between regions. Bent (1939), Packard (1945), Bailey and Niedrach (1965), Burleigh (1972), and Jackman (1975) reported Williamson's sapsuckers nesting primarily in conifers. Other authors (Rasmussen 1941, Hubbard 1965, Tatschl 1967, Ligon 1961, Crockett and Hadow 1975) found a preference for aspens. Of 57 nests in Colorado examined by Crockett and Hadow (1975), 49 were in aspens, especially aspens infected by the Fomes fungus; where pines were used, there were no suitable aspen sites nearby. In Arizona, we found 17 nests in aspen snags, 3 in aspens with dead tops, and 1 nest in a live aspen.

Food: The diet of Williamson's sapsuckers is made up of 87 percent animal and 13 percent vegetable material (Bent 1939). Most of the animal food taken is ants, and most of the vegetable material is cambium. Like the yellow-bellied sapsucker, the Williamson's sapsucker feeds on sap, especially in spring, and picks out "favorite trees" which it taps regularly (Oliver 1970).

44
Hairy woodpecker
Picoides villosus
L 7½″

Habitat: Hairy woodpeckers are residents of nearly all types of forest from central Canada south.

Nest: Live trees in open woodlands are preferred nesting sites of hairy woodpeckers. This species makes a nest entrance that exactly fits its head and body size (1.6 to 1.8 inches). Because this size also seems very convenient for starlings and flying squirrels, hairy woodpeckers are often troubled with invasions (Kilham 1968a, Lawrence 1967). Hairy woodpeckers will often excavate the entrance so it is camouflaged or hidden, such as on the underside of a limb. Nest heights vary from 15 to 45 feet but are commonly approximately 35 feet high. Hairies will often use the same hole year after year.

Food: Hairy woodpeckers prefer to feed on insects on dead and diseased trees (Bent 1939). Approximately 80 percent of the diet is animal matter; adult and larval beetles, ants, and caterpillars are the most frequently eaten items. The primarily insect diet is supplemented with fruit, corn, acorns, hazelnuts, and many other species (Beal 1911, Bent 1939). The males forage in trees away from the nest for large insects (usually borers) located deep in the wood. Females forage close to the nest on the surface of trees, shrubs, or on the ground for small prey (Kilham 1968a).

45
Downy woodpecker
Picoides pubescens
L 5¾″

Habitat: Downy woodpeckers inhabit most of the wooded parts of North America. They are absent or rare in the arid deserts, and not common in the densely forested regions. Favorite habitat includes open woodland, hammocks, orchards, roadside hedges, farmyards, and urban areas (Bent 1939). Occasionally, these birds nest at elevations above 9,000 feet in the central Rockies (Bailey and Niedrach 1965). Most populations are considered nonmigratory; however, there is some movement from north to south and from high elevations to the plains during winter.

Nest: Downy woodpeckers resemble common flickers in many of their nesting habits. Both prefer to excavate near the tops of dead trees in fairly open timber stands. They generally excavate new cavities each year in the same tree, but do not usually use cavities of other birds or reuse old cavities (Lawrence 1967). In the fall, these birds excavate fresh holes to use as winter roosts (Kilham 1962). Nest holes are normally 8 to 50 feet above the ground with an entrance hole 1.2 to 1.4 inches in diameter (Bent 1939).

Food: The diet is about 75 percent animal and 25 percent vegetable material. Animal material consists mostly of economically harmful insects. Kilham (1970) found that beetles, mostly wood-boring larvae, made up 21.5 percent of the diet. Other materials included ants (21 percent), caterpillars (16.5 percent), weevils (3 percent), and fruit (6 percent). Like hairy woodpeckers, downy woodpeckers have been credited with reducing forest pests (MacLellan 1958, 1959, Olson 1953).

46
Ladder-backed woodpecker
Picoides scalaris
L 7″

Habitat: Ladder-backed woodpeckers are commonly found in mesquite and deciduous woodland along streams in desert regions of the Southwest.

Nest: Ladder-backed woodpecker nests are located in a variety of trees such as mesquite, screw bean, palo verde, hackberry, china tree, willow, cottonwood, walnut and oak, usually from 2 to 30 feet above ground. Saguaro cactus, yucca stalks, and branches are sometimes used for nests, as are telephone poles and fence posts (Bent 1939, Phillips et al. 1964).

Food: Insects, especially larvae of wood-boring beetles, caterpillars, and ants, are major food items. The ladder-backed woodpecker also has been reported to eat the ripe fruit of saguaro cactus (Bent 1939).

47
Nuttall's woodpecker
Picoides nuttallii
L 6¾″

Habitat: This western woodpecker is an inhabitant of oak woodlands, riparian woods, and chapparal west of the Sierras in California.

Nest: From a literature survey and personal observations, Miller and Bock (1972) summarized the following nest-tree data for 57 nests: 23 percent in oak, 19 percent in willow, 18 percent in sycamore, 16 percent in cottonwood, and 12 percent in alder. Cavities were excavated in dead limbs and trunks of trees, from 3 to 45 feet above ground.

Food: About 80 percent of the diet of Nuttall's woodpecker is insects, including 28 percent beetles, 15 percent hemipterans, 14 percent lepidopteran larvae, and 8 percent ants (Beal 1911). Most of the insects are gleaned from trunk and limb surfaces or captured on the wing (Short 1971). Wild fruits, poison oak seeds, and occasional acorns make up the vegetable portion of the diet. Nuttall's woodpeckers in California have been known to take almonds, occasionally robbing the caches of Lewis' woodpeckers (Emlen 1937, Bock 1970).

48

Arizona woodpecker
Picoides arizonae
L 7¼"

Habitat: Arizona woodpeckers are found in live oak and oak-pine forests and canyons from 4,000 to 7,500 feet in Arizona and New Mexico.

Nest: The Arizona woodpecker excavates holes in dead branches of living trees, primarily walnuts, oaks, maples, and sycamores. One nest was reportedly located in a mescal stalk (Bent 1939).

Food: This woodpecker's diet probably consists largely of the adult and larval stages of insects, with some fruit and acorns, but few details of food items have been reported (Bent 1939).

49
Red-cockaded woodpecker
Picoides borealis
7¼"

Habitat: Red-cockaded woodpeckers need open, mature (at least 60 year old) pine forest with a high fire occurrence (Bent 1939, Jackson 1971, Hopkins and Lynn 1971). Pine species used during breeding season include: longleaf (Crosby 1971), slash (Lowry 1960), loblolly (Sprunt and Chamberlain 1949), and shortleaf (Sutton 1967). Red-cockaded woodpeckers are on the national "Endangered species" list.

Nest: These woodpeckers prefer living pines infected with red heart rot for nesting. These trees have a soft, easily excavated interior with a living exterior, leaving the tree less susceptible to destruction by fire than a dead tree. Cavities can often be reused for at least 20 years and for several years by the same pair (Ligon 1971). The height of cavity is influenced by the location of red heart infection and the height and density of undergrowth (Crosby 1971). The majority of cavities face west, and, when found in leaning trees, are generally on the low side (Beckett 1971, Baker 1971).

Food: Insects make up the major portion of the diet of red-cockaded woodpeckers. Beal (1911) and Beal et al. (1916) examined 99 stomachs and found 86 percent insects and 14 percent vegetable matter, mostly mast. Beetle larvae (16 percent) and ants made up an important part of the year-round diet. The corn earworm can be a major food source during several weeks where conditions are suitable (Ward 1930). Plant material recorded being eaten includes wax myrtle, magnolia, poison ivy, wild grape, pokeberry, blueberry, wild cherry, black gum, and pecan (Beal 1911, Baker 1971, Ligon 1971).

50
White-headed woodpecker
Picoides albolarvatus
L 7¾"

Habitat: Open ponderosa pine forest from Washington to central California is the primary habitat of the white-headed woodpecker, but it also occurs in sugar pine, Jeffrey pine, and red and white fir forests (Grinnell and Miller 1944).

Nest: This woodpecker seems to prefer dead pines, but nests have also been found in live and dead fir, oak, and aspen. White-headed woodpeckers usually excavate a new nest cavity every year and often excavate several holes before selecting one to nest in (Bent 1939). Average nest height is 8 feet above ground.

Food: White-headed woodpeckers feed primarily on pine seeds during the winter and early spring, and on insects during the summer. Tevis (1953) determined that 60 percent of the annual diet was pine seeds and 40 percent was insects. Ants made up half of the insect food; other insects taken were woodboring beetles, spiders, and fly larvae (Beal 1911, Grinnell and Storer 1924, Ligon 1973).

51
Black-backed three-toed woodpecker
Picoides arcticus
L 8″

Habitat: The conifer forests of the north are preferred, but this three-toed woodpecker is not abundant even in its favorite habitat. Forest types include mixed conifer, lodgepole pine, white fir, subalpine fir, tamarack swamps, boreal spruce-balsam fir, Douglas-fir, and mixed hardwood-conifer.

Nest: This species usually excavates its cavities in snags or live trees with dead heartwood, especially in areas that have been burned or logged (Bent 1939). Nests are usually in spruce, balsam fir, pines, or Douglas-fir, although maple, birch, and cedar have been used.

Food: The food of this species is similar to that of the northern three-toed woodpecker. Beal (1911) found 75 percent of the food to be woodboring beetle larvae, mainly long-horned beetles and metallic woodboring beetles. Weevils and other beetles, spiders, and ants are eaten along with some wild fruit, mast, and cambium. Beal estimated that each three-toed woodpecker annually consumed 13,675 woodboring beetle larvae.

52
Northern three-toed woodpecker
Picoides tridactylus
L 7½″

Habitat: This highly beneficial woodpecker is most common in coniferous forests of the West, but does occur occasionally in the Northeast.

Nest: The northern three-toed woodpecker excavates nest cavities each year in standing dead trees or in dead limbs of live trees with rotted heartwood (Jackman and Scott 1975). Their nest cavities have been reported in pine, aspen, spruce, and cedar trees (Bent 1939). In Arizona, we found two nests in ponderosa pine snags.

Food: The northern three-toed woodpecker is probably one of the most important birds in combating forest insect pests in the western United States. Massey and Wygant (1973) found that spruce beetles comprised 65 percent of their diet in Colorado. During the winter when other foods were scarce, the spruce beetle made up 99 percent of the food taken. West and Speiers (1959) reported that both species of three-toed woodpeckers in northeastern United States feed on elm bark beetles, which carry Dutch elm disease. Koplin (1972) estimated that 20 percent of an endemic and 84 percent of an epidemic spruce beetle population in Colorado were consumed by three species of woodpeckers, the most important of which was the northern three-toed. Other foods include ants, woodboring and lepidopteran larvae, fruits, mast, and cambium (Beal 1911, Massey and Wygant 1973).

53
Ivory-billed woodpecker
Campephilus principalis
L 18″

Habitat: Cooke (1888) and Bent (1939) described the largest of the North American woodpeckers as rare, shy, and found only in the heaviest timber in virgin cypress and bottomland forest of the South. Tanner (1942) described ivory-billed woodpecker habitat as heavily forested and usually flooded alluvial land bordering rivers, made up of oaks, cypress, and green ash. The most recent sightings (between 5 and 10 pairs) have been made in bottomland hardwoods that have been cut over but still have some large, mature trees (Dennis 1967). They are included on the national "Endangered species" list.

Nest: Nest cavities of this species have been recorded in almost every species of tree occurring within the ivory-bill's habitat (Greenway 1958). The squarish holes (Dennis 1967) are high, 16 to 65 feet, and in the trunks of living or dead trees (Greenway 1958, Forbush and May 1939).

Food: Ivory-billed woodpeckers could be of economic importance except for their small numbers (Greenway 1958). The woodboring larvae making up a third of their diet (Beal 1911) are injurious to trees (Pearson 1936), and are most abundant in areas where recently dead and dying trees are numerous because of flooding, fire, insect attacks, or storms. The birds stay as long as there are abundant larvae (Dennis 1967). They also eat fruit of magnolia and pecan trees (Beal 1911).

54
Sulphur-bellied flycatcher
Myiodynastes luteiventris
L 6¾″

Habitat: The sulphur-bellied flycatcher is a common occupant of riparian habitat with sycamore trees in deep canyons from 5,000 to 7,500 feet elevation in the Huachuca Mountains of Arizona.

Nest: Invariably the nest of this species, made from leaf stems (Peterson 1961), is built in a natural cavity in a large sycamore at a height between 20 and 50 feet above the ground. The cavity normally is a knothole where a large branch has broken off (Bent 1942). At least one member of each pair may return to the same nest site each year.

Food: Little information has been published on the food habits of this flycatcher, but insects caught in the air are undoubtedly the major items. Apparently small fruits and berries also are eaten (Bent 1942).

55
Great crested flycatcher
Myiarchus crinitus
L 7"

Habitat: Great crested flycatchers are common in deciduous and mixed woods east of the Rockies. They were originally a deep forest bird, but with increases in forest clearing and thinning operations, fewer and fewer cavities are available. They seem to be adapting well to less densely forested areas, areas treated with herbicides, and forest-field edge situations (Hespenheide 1971, Bent 1942).

Nest: Great crested flycatchers use natural cavities or excavations made by other species. Nests are found in a variety of tree species anywhere from 3 to 70 feet above the ground (mostly below 20 feet). They build a bulky nest, and therefore prefer deep cavities. Before constructing a nest, they will generally fill a deep cavity with trash to a level of 12 to 18 inches from the top. They are well known for their habit of including a snake skin in the nest or dangling it from the cavity opening (Bent 1942).

Food: Food habit studies have shown that great crested flycatchers eat 94 percent animal and 6 percent vegetable material. Most frequently eaten are butterflies, beetles, grasshoppers, crickets, katydids, bees, and sawflies. Vegetable matter is mainly wild fruits. Most food is caught in flight in the usual flycatcher fashion (Bent 1942).

56
Wied's crested flycatcher
Myiarchus tyrannulus
L 7¼"

Habitat: Desert saguaros, deciduous woodlands and riparian vegetation in the Southwest are the preferred habitats of the Wied's crested flycatcher.

Nest: Nests made from twigs, weeds, and trash are built in abandoned woodpecker holes in saguaro cacti at a height from 5 to 20 feet above the ground. Sycamores, cottonwoods, and fence posts are used occasionally (Bent 1942).

Food: The diet of this species is similar to that of other crested flycatchers, consisting mostly of beetles, flying insects, and perhaps some berries and fruits (Bent 1942).

57
Ash-throated flycatcher
Myiarchus cinerascens

L 6½"

Habitat: The ash-throated flycatcher occupies dense mesquite thickets, oak groves, saguaro cactus, riparian vegetation, and pinyon juniper forests. It ranges from Washington to the southwestern United States and Texas.

Nest: The ash-throated flycatcher is not particularly specific in tree selection as long as it has a cavity. Woodpecker holes, exposed pipes, and nest boxes have been used. Mesquite, ash, oak, sycamore, juniper, and cottonwood are common nest trees (Bent 1942).

Food: The diet of this species consists mainly of animal material. Beetles, bees, wasps, bugs, flies, caterpillars, moths, grasshoppers, spiders, etc., make up about 92 percent of the diet. Mistletoe, berries, and other fleshy fruits account for the remainder (Bent 1942).

58
Olivaceous flycatcher
Myiarchus tuberculifer
L 5¾"

Habitat: Olivaceous flycatchers are found in dense oak thickets, pinyon-juniper forests, and along canyon streams in Arizona and southwestern New Mexico.

Nest: Nests are located in natural cavities or abandoned woodpecker holes. Oaks are preferred, but nests also have been reported in ash and sycamore trees (Bent 1942).

Food: Limited evidence on food habits of this species indicates that the major food items are small insects including grasshoppers, termites, mayflies, treehoppers, miscellaneous bugs, moths, bees, wasps, and spiders (Bent 1942).

59
Western flycatcher
Empidonax difficilis
L 5"

Habitat: Moist deciduous or coniferous forests and areas near running water with tall trees are favored by the western flycatcher (Grinnell and Miller 1944).

Nest: Western flycatchers sometimes nest in cavities, but use a variety of nest sites. Davis et al. (1963) found four nests in natural cavities in willows and oaks, and six behind flaps of bark in sycamores and willows. Nests are often reported in natural rock crevices, on tree limbs and crotches, and on ledges of buildings (Bent 1942, Davis et al. 1963, Beaver 1967).

Food: Almost all of the food of the western flycatcher is insects captured on the wing. An examination of 23 stomachs showed 31 percent flies, 25 percent beetles, 23 percent lepidopterans (including pupae and adults of spruce budworms), and 17 percent hymenopterans (Beaver 1967).

60
Violet-green swallow
Tachycineta thalassina
L 4¾"

Habitat: Ponderosa pine affords the favorite habitat for violet-green swallows (Bailey and Niedrach 1965), but they are also found in aspen-willow and spruce-aspen forests. They prefer open or broken woods or the edges of dense forests.

Nest: Violet-green swallows nest in holes, cavities, and crevices in a variety of situations. Where birds are abundant, the demand for nest sites is sometimes greater than the supply, and practically any available cavity may be used. These swallows have been reported to use old nests of cliff swallows and even burrows of bank swallow (Bent 1942). Winternitz (1973) reported violet-greens using old woodpecker holes in live aspen as nesting sites, but in Arizona, we found them nesting primarily in old woodpecker holes in ponderosa pine snags. We found one in the dead top of an aspen, 5 in dead tops of ponderosa pine, and 26 in ponderosa pine snags. Nest heights ranged from 16 to 80 feet and averaged 43 feet.

Food: Apparently, the diet of this species is exclusively insects taken on the wing. It includes leafhoppers, leaf bugs, flies, flying ants, and some wasps, bees, and beetles (Bent 1942). In Colorado, Baldwin (pers. comm.[7]) found that insects made up 99 percent of the stomach contents of six violet-green swallows. Flies were the most abundant insect found. Scolytid beetles, seed and leaf bugs, miscellaneous insects, and a few spiders were also found.

61
Tree swallow
Iridoprocne bicolor
L 5"

Habitat: Tree swallows breed throughout North America from the northern half of the United States north to the limit of tree growth. They are migrants throughout the Central and Southern states and winter primarily in Central America.

Nest: Tree swallows prefer to nest in natural cavities and old woodpecker holes—usually near water. The lack of natural cavities, competition for existing cavities, and the availability of nest boxes, have resulted in a shift in nesting preferences to nest boxes in the eastern United States (Bent 1942, Low 1933, Whittle 1926). Bluebird boxes and purple martin houses are frequently used. Tree swallows are not colonial, but will nest within 7 feet of each other, if there are adequate meadows, marsh, or water area available for feeding (Whittle 1926). Woodpecker holes in aspen, spruce, and pine are the most common nest sites in the West (Bailey and Niedrach 1965).

Food: This species is the first of the swallows to arrive in the north in the spring, and the last to depart in the fall. Because tree swallows can subsist on seeds and berries, they are not as dependent upon insects as are other swallows. They are partial to waxmyrtle and bayberry where these are available. Plant food proportions in the diet are 1 percent in spring, 21 percent in summer, 29 percent in fall, and 30 percent in winter (Martin et al. 1951, Forbush and May 1939).

62
Purple martin
Progne subis
L 7″

Habitat: The natural nesting population of purple martins prefer open woodlands or cutover forests where suitable snags remain. Purple martins have been reported in oak, sycamore, ponderosa pine, Monterey pine, spruce, and fir forests of California (Grinnell and Miller 1944). In the Southwest, the purple martin breeds in the ponderosa pine belt and in the saguaro cactus desert.

Nest: The western purple martin has not adapted to nesting in boxes as well as the eastern form (Bunch 1964), and much of the western population depends upon holes made by woodpeckers, usually in tall pines in relatively open timber stands (Bent 1942). Martins also nest in old woodpecker holes in saguaro cactus. We have recorded 21 nests near Cibecue, Arizona, all in ponderosa pine snags. Nests ranged from 25 to 35 feet above ground. Nest compartments in martin houses should be 6 × 6 × 6 inches with an entrance hole 2½ inches in diameter 1 inch above the floor. The boxes should be 15 to 20 feet above ground.

Food: The purple martin feeds on the wing, and nearly all the diet is insects, although some spiders are taken (Beal 1918). Johnston (1967) examined the stomach contents of 34 martins collected in April, May, June, and August in Kansas. Beetles, true bugs, flies, bees, and wasps were the important food items. Although the purple martin has been credited for feeding on large numbers of mosquitoes (Bent 1942), it was not documented by the two food habit studies mentioned.

63
Black-capped chickadee
Parus atricapillus
L 4½″

Habitat: Black-capped chickadees nest throughout southern Canada and the northern half of the United States. In Missouri, the black-capped chickadee generally nests north of the Missouri River and the Carolina chickadee nests south of the River. The breeding range extends farther south at higher elevations of the Rocky and Appalachian Mountain ranges than in non-mountainous areas. In Colorado, black-caps are most abundant in the ponderosa pine and aspen forests (Bailey and Niedrach 1965).

Nest: Chickadees nest in cavities but roost anywhere convenient, generally not in cavities (Odum 1942). The most suitable nesting sites are stubs with partially decayed cores and firm shells. They usually excavate their own cavities, but will use natural cavities or nest boxes. Black-caps will occasionally nest in a cavity they used the previous year after making some alterations. Preferred nesting sites throughout the eastern forests are tree species that occur in the early seral stages but that are short lived and persist in the intermediate stages as decaying stubs (Odum 1941, Brewer 1961).

Food: The diet of the black-capped chickadee is comprised of 70 percent animal and 30 percent vegetable matter. Mast, chiefly from coniferous trees, and fruits of bayberry, blackberry, blueberry, and poison ivy make up the bulk of the vegetable matter. Animal material eaten (mostly insects) includes caterpillars, eggs, moths, spiders, and beetles. Winter diet is primarily larvae, eggs, katydids, and spiders (Bent 1946, Martin et al. 1951).

64
Carolina chickadee
Parus carolinensis
L 4¼"

Habitat: The Carolina chickadee, which inhabits the southeastern forests, is a slightly smaller version of the black-capped chickadee. In Missouri, the Carolina chickadee nests south of the Missouri River throughout the Ozarks.

Nest: The nesting habits of the black-capped and Carolina chickadees are quite similar. They occasionally nest in natural cavities or deserted holes of woodpeckers, but commonly excavate their own nest cavity in decaying wood of dead trunks or limbs of deciduous trees (Bent 1946). Black-capped and Carolina chickadees line their nesting cavities with fine grasses and feathers.

Food: Food habits of the Carolina chickadee are also very similar to those of the black-capped chickadee. Food consists of insects and a variety of fleshy fruits and seeds (Bent 1946).

65
Mexican chickadee
Parus sclateri
L 4¼"

Habitat: This species inhabits pine and spruce forests from 7,000 to 10,000 feet elevation just inside the United States in the Chiricahua Mountains of Arizona and the Animas Mountains of New Mexico (Phillips et al. 1964).

Nest: Mexican chickadees excavate nest holes in dead trees or branches. One nest was found in a willow stub about 5 feet above the ground (Bent 1946).

Food: No information on diet was found in the literature.

66
Mountain chickadee
Parus gambeli
L 4¼"

Habitat: This common little chickadee can be found in most coniferous forests of the West from 6,000 to 11,000 feet (Bent 1946).

Nest: Mountain chickadees usually nest in natural cavities or abandoned woodpecker holes, and probably do not excavate their own cavities if suitable ones are available (Bent 1946). Winternitz (1973) reported five nests in live aspen and one in a dead aspen, 6 to 15 feet above ground. In Arizona, we have found five nests in live aspen, three in aspen snags, two in ponderosa pine snags, and one in a white fir snag.

Food: Insects probably make up a large portion of the diet (Bent 1946). Telford and Herman (1963) collected 10 birds in the Inyo National Forest, where there was an infestation of lodgepole needle miners and found 639 needle miner caterpillars in chickadee stomachs. Baldwin (pers. comm.[8]) examined the contents of 17 stomachs from the Wet Mountains, Colorado, and found that 75 percent of the summer diet was insects. Large numbers of spruce aphids were found, as well as flies, beetles, hymenopterans, and other insects. Vegetable material included seeds, spruce buds, and fruits. In southwestern Montana, during summer, mountain chickadees fed on lepidopteran larvae, especially cone worms and spruce budworms (DeWeese et al.[9][in prep.]), and insects made up about 98 percent of the diet.

67
Gray-headed chickadee
Parus cinctus
L $4\frac{3}{4}''$

Habitat: Broken forests or edges of aspen, willow, and spruce are the preferred habitat of the gray-headed chickadee. The range is limited to western Canada and Alaska.

Nest: Old woodpecker holes or natural cavities are selected as nest sites. Bent (1946) reported one nest about 6 feet above ground in a spruce snag.

Food: No information could be found in the literature on the food habits of the gray-headed chickadee, but the diet is probably similar to that of other chickadees.

68
Boreal chickadee
Parus hudsonicus
L $4\frac{1}{4}''$

Habitat: The boreal chickadee is fairly common in northern forests of spruce, fir, aspen, and birch (McLaren 1975).

Nest: Natural cavities, old woodpecker holes, or cavities excavated by the chickadees themselves are used for nesting (Bent 1946). McLaren (1975) found 22 nest holes, all in trees or snags with soft heartwood, and believed that softness of the core rather than a preference for a certain tree species is the determining factor in nest site selection.

Food: In summer the boreal chickadee consumes caterpillars, moths, beetles, other insects, and insect eggs; birch cones, seeds, and cedar berries are eaten in the fall and winter (Bent 1946).

69

Chestnut-backed chickadee
Parus rufescens
L 4¼″

Habitat: Coniferous forests of the humid coastal belt from Alaska to central California are the favorite habitat, but this bird is also found in adjacent deciduous woodlands and along streams (Peterson 1961, Grinnell and Miller 1944).

Nest: Nests of this species are in abandoned woodpecker holes or in cavities excavated by the bird itself. Nests have been found in pine, oak, and Douglas-fir snags (Bent 1946).

Food: The diet is made up of about 65 percent animal and 35 percent vegetable matter. Of the animal material, 25 percent is hemipterans, 18 percent caterpillars, 13 percent wasps, 7 percent spiders, and 2 percent beetles. Seeds and fruit make up the vegetable material (Beal 1907).

70
Tufted titmouse
Parus bicolor
L 5½″

Habitat: The tufted titmouse is the largest North American titmouse and is common throughout the eastern deciduous woodlands. These active and vocal birds are generally found in groups of 2 to 6 in thick timber stands, often near water (Gillespie 1930). The black-crested titmouse, found in southern Texas and northeastern Mexico, is now considered conspecific with the tufted titmouse (33rd supplement, A.O.U. Checklist).

Nest: Nests of the tufted titmouse are very difficult to locate and are not often reported in the literature. Published accounts indicate that these birds nest in abandoned woodpecker holes or natural cavities usually less than 20 feet above the ground. While titmice are quite conspicuous in late fall and winter, they tend to disappear in late spring to nest and molt (Gillespie 1930, Laskey 1957).

Food: The diets of tufted titmice change seasonally. In spring and summer they eat primarily animal matter (89 percent and 82 percent respectively) and spend most of their feeding time in the tree tops. Caterpillars often make up over 50 percent of the animal matter. Common winter foods consist of beechnuts, acorns, dogwood berries, Virginia creeper berries, alder seeds, honeysuckle, seeds of tulip-tree pods. In winter, they spend a larger percentage of their feeding time on or near the ground (Gillespie 1930, Martin et al. 1951).

71
Plain titmouse
Parus inornatus
L 5″

Habitat: Oak and pinyon-juniper woodlands from 5,000 to 7,000 feet elevation from Oregon south and west to Texas and New Mexico are the favored habitat of the plain titmouse.

Nest: Plain titmice usually nest in natural cavities or old woodpecker holes. Most reported nests have been in oaks, 2 to 23 feet above ground (Bent 1946). Nest boxes are used when available (Wetmore 1964).

Food: Beal (Bent 1946) examined the contents of 76 stomachs and found 43 percent animal material (true bugs 12 percent, caterpillars 11 percent, beetles 7 percent, ants and wasps 6 percent, daddy longlegs and grasshoppers 5 percent, spiders 1 percent, and 1 percent unreported) and 57 percent vegetable matter (cherries and pulp of larger fruit and leaf galls 32 percent, seeds of poison oak and weeds 25 percent).

72
Bridled titmouse
Parus wollweberi
L 4½"

Habitat: Bridled titmice prefer chaparral and pinyon-juniper in the Southwest at elevations from 5,000 to 7,000 feet. This titmouse also uses areas along streams where cottonwoods are present (Phillips et al. 1964).

Nest: Almost all nest locations have been recorded in natural cavities of dead and living oak trees from 4 to 28 feet above the ground (Bent 1946).

Food: No published information was found, but the diet is probably similar to that of other members of this genus. All live in similar habitats and spend much of their time foraging in crevices in the bark, on the trunks, and on branches, presumably hunting for adults, larvae, and eggs of insects (Bent 1946).

73
White-breasted nuthatch
Sitta carolinensis
L 5"

Habitat: White-breasted nuthatches are non-migratory in most forest types in the United States. They show a preference for deciduous woodlands. In the Rocky Mountains, they occur most commonly below 9,500 feet elevation (Bailey and Niedrach 1965).

Nest: White-breasted nuthatches nest almost exclusively in natural cavities within living trees of mature forests. When natural cavities are unavailable, they may use an abandoned woodpecker hole (Kilham 1968b). In the West, nests have been found in dead aspens and dead portions (lightning strikes) of live ponderosa pines (Bailey and Niedrach 1965, Scott and Patton 1975). Nests are lined with hair and feathers and are often used for more than 1 year.

Food: A myriad of insects, including larvae of the gypsy moth and the forest tent caterpillar, beetles, spiders, caterpillars, and ants comprise the main diet of white-breasted nuthatches throughout the spring and summer. In the winter, nearly all food eaten is mast composed of beechnuts, acorns, hickory nuts, maize and sunflower seeds (Bent 1948). Among the insect foods are several other forest pests including nut weevils, locust seed weevils, and roundheaded woodborers (Scott and Patton 1975). Nuthatches may also be attracted to feeders with suet and sunflower seeds.

74
Red-breasted nuthatch
Sitta canadensis
L 4″

Habitat: Red-breasted nuthatches nest throughout the high elevations of the Rocky Mountains and in the Canadian boreal forests. They are erratic winter migrants to the eastern forest types. In Colorado, their preferred habitat is the coniferous-aspen type from the Canadian Life Zone to timberline.

Nest: Red-breasted nuthatches will excavate their own cavity if a natural cavity or woodpecker hole is not available or to their liking (de Kiriline 1952). Nests are usually 6 to 40 feet above the ground in rotten stubs or branches of dead trees. Nests have been reported in birch, poplar, cottonwood, oak, and pine. Nests usually are not lined, in contrast to those of white-breasted nuthatches.

Food: Little is known of the food taken by red-breasted nuthatches. They feed on seeds of pine, spruce, and other coniferous trees. The animal food is known to include beetles, hymenoptera, spiders, and ribbed pine borers. They sometimes feed on flying insects (Bent 1948). Birds will visit feeders offering suet during the winter.

75
Brown-headed nuthatch
Sitta pusilla
L 3½″

Habitat: Clearings and areas that have been burned (more old stumps available for nesting) in southern pine woods are preferred by brown-headed nuthatches. They can also be found in mixed pine and hardwood forests of extreme southeastern United States (Bent 1948).

Nest: Brown-headed nuthatches excavate or partially excavate nest cavities 4.5 to 8 inches deep in dead trees and stumps (often fire blackened) or posts and poles. Bent (1948) gave little evidence that the brown-headed nuthatch will use old woodpecker holes, but they may enlarge and use natural cavities. The nests are located 3 to 46 feet from the ground (only rarely above 13 feet). Because nest entrances are more like a crack in a tree than rounded like a woodpecker hole, nests are difficult to find (Pearson 1936).

Food: Brown-headed nuthatches are mainly insectivorous, and are considered a useful protector of trees. They search for insects and their eggs in crevices of the bark on the trunks, branches, twigs, and needles of pines. They also eat pine seeds (Bent 1948).

76
Pygmy nuthatch
Sitta pygmaea
L 3½"

Habitat: Pygmy nuthatches are common in ponderosa pine forests throughout the West. They are also found in Jeffrey pine, Bishop pine, and Monterey pine associations in California (Grinnell and Miller 1944), and in pinyon-juniper woodlands in Arizona (Phillips et al. 1964).

Nest: Nearly all reported nests of the pygmy nuthatch have been from 8 to 60 feet above ground in cavities excavated by the bird itself in dead or live pine trees (Bent 1948). We found 27 nests in ponderosa pine snags and two in dead aspens in the White Mountains of Arizona.

Food: About 80 percent of the diet is animal material, mostly wasps and spittle insects, including some ants, beetles, and caterpillars; the balance is nearly all conifer seeds (Bent 1948).

77
Brown creeper
Certhia familiaris
L 4¾"

Habitat: This inconspicuous small bird is fairly common in the coniferous forests of the Transition and Canadian Life Zones. In Colorado, it breeds from 7,000 feet to timberline (Bailey and Neidrach 1965). Creepers winter throughout the forests of the southern states.

Nest: Sometimes creepers nest in natural cavities and old woodpecker holes, but generally they make their nests between the loose bark and the trunk of a large dead tree (Bent 1948). We found three nests behind the loosened bark of dead ponderosa pines and one in a white fir snag in the White Mountains of Arizona.

Food: Few details are known, but the diet is mainly insects, including weevils, leafhoppers, flat bugs, jumping plant lice, scale insects, eggs of katydids, ants and other small hymenoptera, sawflies, moths, caterpillars, cocoons of leaf skeletonizers, pupae of the codling moth, spiders, and pseudoscorpions (Bent 1948). The small amount of vegetable material eaten is chiefly mast.

78
House wren
Troglodytes aedon
L 4¼"

Habitat: House wrens are common nesters in shrubbery and brush throughout the northern two-thirds of the United States, but they winter in the southern states. They range from the plains to timberline throughout the Rocky Mountains. They are commonly found along the edges of woods, swamps, fields, and in orchards.

Nest: House wrens are aggressive in their nesting habits and will drive other birds from cavities. Nests have been found in a variety of sites including 2-inch pipes used to brace fence posts, nesting boxes, natural cavities, and downy woodpecker holes (Sutton 1930). Nests are usually less than 10 feet above the ground. Diameter of the entrance hole in nesting boxes should be 1 inch.

Food: House wrens are capable of eating large quantities of insects and arthropods, which constitute 98 percent of their diet. Animal items include beetles, caterpillars, bugs, grasshoppers, and ants (Bent 1948).

79
Brown-throated wren
Troglodytes brunneicollis
L 4″

Habitat: Brown-throated wrens inhabit oak forests, mostly in desert ranges, but can be found up to elevations of 8,000 feet in southern Arizona.

Nest: This wren uses natural cavities or old woodpecker holes in tree trunks or limbs. Like the house wren, it will sometimes occupy recesses about buildings and nest boxes (Pough 1957).

Food: We could not find published information on food habits but the diet is probably insects similar to that of other wrens.

80
Winter wren
Troglodytes troglodytes
L 3¼″

Habitat: Winter wrens inhabit coniferous forests of spruce, fir, and pine, and underbrush in woodlands in eastern and western United States and Canada.

Nest: Winter wren nests, made from twigs and leaves, are built near the ground in exposed roots or fallen logs or in rocks and crevices (Bent 1948, Wetmore 1964).

Food: Details on food items were not found in the literature, but the diet is probably adult and larval stages of insects (Bent 1948).

81
Bewick's wren
Thryomanes bewickii
L 4½″

Habitat: Bewick's wrens are common and widespread in the West, but uncommon and local in the Appalachians and Ozarks. They are usually found in farmyards, brushlands, fencerows, and suburban areas. Bewick's wrens are fairly common in the pinyon-juniper forest type, and in mesquite-willow-cottonwood associations along southwestern streams.

Nest: Nests of the Bewick's wren can be found in a multitude of places. Most nests are cup-shaped and can be either open or closed above. They are usually located in cavities close to the ground (Miller 1941). Nest sites include natural cavities, woodpecker holes, knotholes in fallen trees, fence posts, tin cans, bird boxes, and deserted automobiles (Bent 1948).

Food: Bewick's wrens, like other wrens, eat large numbers of insects that are injurious to vegetation. Ninety-seven percent of the diet is insects, including primarily hemiptera and coleoptera. In the South they are credited with eating boll weevils (Bent 1948).

82
Carolina wren
Thryothorus ludovicianus
L 4¾″

Habitat: Carolina wrens are common in forest types with thick underbrush throughout the eastern United States. The number in northern populations fluctuates widely depending on the harshness of winter conditions.

Nest: Carolina wrens are quite universal in their choice of nesting sites. These wrens prefer nesting sites that are fairly well enclosed, but they are not totally dependent upon cavities. They are well adapted to habitat conditions provided by man, but also nest in the woods where they prefer tangles and brushy undergrowth. Nests have been found in natural cavities, mailboxes, newspaper cylinders, old hornet nests, and bird houses (Laskey 1948, Nice and Thomas 1948).

Food: Animal food, mostly insects, makes up 93 percent of the Carolina wren's diet. Of this, beetles, caterpillars, and moths comprise the largest portion. The 7 percent vegetable material is mostly seeds taken in the winter. Since the Carolina wren feeds mostly on or near the ground, deep snow is detrimental to survival. They will visit feeding stations if placed near brush piles (Bent 1948).

83
Eastern bluebird
Sialia sialis
L 5½″

Habitat: Under natural conditions, eastern bluebirds prefer to use cavities in savannah-like habitats east of the Great Plains (Rustad 1972). They are an edge species and therefore do not live in dense woods or in closely built residential sections of town (Thomas 1946). Like purple martins, bluebirds have taken advantage of nest boxes provided in areas around farms, near open fields, and in orchards.

Nest: Eastern bluebird nesting sites (snags) are often eliminated because of their unsightliness or interference with cultivation. When available, eastern bluebirds nest in old woodpecker holes, hollows of decayed trees, and crevices of rocks (Pearson 1936). They will readily take to hollows in wooden fence posts or correctly sized and placed nest boxes (5 × 5 × 8 inches high with a 1.5-inch hole located 6 inches from the bottom). Boxes should be placed 5 to 10 feet above the ground at the edge of a forest opening or field.

Food: Eastern bluebirds consume 70 percent animal matter and 30 percent vegetable matter. Vegetable intake increases to more than 50 percent in December and January, but is completely lacking in May. Animal matter includes grasshoppers, crickets and katydids, various coleoptera, moths and caterpillars, some hymenoptera and hemiptera, as well as various other invertebrates and small vertebrates. Vegetable matter is mostly wild fruits (Bent 1949).

84
Western bluebird
Sialia mexicana
L 5½″

Habitat: The western bluebird is most abundant in open ponderosa pine forests of the Transition Zone, but may also be found in oak woodlands, pinyon-juniper, mixed conifer, and subalpine forests.

Nest: Nests are usually in old woodpecker holes, but this bird also uses natural cavities. Nests have been reported in oak, sycamore, and pine trees. In Monterey County, California, nests were found from 5 to 40 feet above ground in pine stumps or trees (Bent 1949). This bluebird, like the eastern, also readily nests near humans in bird houses. Nest boxes should be 5 × 5 × 8 inches with a 1.5-inch entrance hole located 6 inches from the floor. Boxes should be placed 5 to 10 feet above ground near forest openings or meadows.

Food: Beal (Bent 1949) examined the contents of 217 stomachs and found 72 percent animal material (grasshoppers 21 percent, caterpillars 20 percent, useful beetles 9 percent, other beetles 16 percent, ants 5 percent, other hymenoptera 1 percent) and 28 percent vegetable material, mostly wild fruits, including elderberries, mistletoe berries, blackberries or raspberries, prunes, cherries, and a few weed seeds.

85
Mountain bluebird
Sialia currucoides
L 6″

Habitat: The mountain bluebird nests in nearly all timber types of the Rocky Mountain region, and is reported from 800 to 11,000 feet elevation in Idaho (Burleigh 1972). However, this species usually ranges from 7,000 to 11,000 feet in open forests or near forest edges.

Nest: The mountain bluebird usually nests in natural cavities or in old woodpecker holes but will also use man-made structures. Nests have been reported in fir and pinyon snags and aspen trees (Burleigh 1972, Bent 1949). We recorded six nests in the White Mountains of Arizona ranging from 12 to 35 feet above ground in ponderosa pine snags. Five of these were in abandoned woodpecker holes and one was in a natural cavity. Nest boxes should be similar to those for other bluebirds.

Food: This is probably the most insectivorous of the bluebirds. Studies indicate that nearly 92 percent of the diet is animal material, including miscellaneous beetles, weevils, ants, bees, wasps, cicadas, stinkbugs, negro bugs, assassin bugs, jassids, flies, caterpillars, grasshoppers, locusts, and crickets (Bent 1949). Vegetable items include currants, grapes, elderberries, sumac seeds, mistletoe berries, hackberry seeds, Virginia creeper seeds, and cedar berries.

86
Starling
Sturnus vulgaris
L 6″

Habitat: Starlings breed in various habitats that provide adequate nestling food (Troetschler 1976) but are perhaps most numerous in suburban and rural habitat where suitable nesting sites abound. Kalmbach (1928) noted that starlings prefer thickly settled agricultural areas and stated that "They are partial to human association...." During establishment in the United States, starlings first settled in lowland areas and are still abundant there (Small 1974, Royall 1966, Bent 1950). In a southeast Ontario test, starlings preferred old field habitat over five other habitats when sufficient nest sites were available (Gibo et al. 1976).

Nest: Cavities in trees, telephone poles, or fence posts, in drainpipes, mail boxes, or buildings, and in haystacks and cliffs have been used for nesting, as have burrows and open nests of other species (Kessel 1957, Bent 1950). Natural nest sites seem to be preferred over nest boxes (Planck 1967). Competition between starlings and native species for nesting cavities usually favors the starling, but most native species seem to breed in some habitats where starlings are not numerous.

Food: Analysis of contents of 2,750 starling stomachs taken in the northeastern states showed 57 percent animal materials such as insects, millipeds, spiders, molluscs, and a few crustaceans. Insects such as weevils, ground beetles, and plant-feeding scarabaeids such as May beetles were especially important. Of the 43 percent vegetable material, wild fruit was most important, but cultivated cherries, vegetable material, grain, and seeds of various sorts were also used (Kalmbach 1928). In other areas, grapes, blueberries, figs, and other fruit, truck crops, sprouting crops, and prepared livestock feed are eaten.

87
Crested myna
Acridotheres cristatellus
L 9″

Habitat: The crested myna is native to the plains and lowlands of cultivated southern China, and was introduced in Vancouver, B.C., Canada in the 1890's. Although the myna has been reported in the states of Washington and Oregon, most of the population is in Greater Vancouver and Vancouver Island. Mynas are apparently dwellers of urban and nearby open field areas (Mackay and Hughes 1963).

Nest: In urban areas, mynas nest in almost any enclosed area, including bird boxes intended for other birds. In wooded areas, holes made by flickers and other woodpeckers seem to be preferred (Bent 1950).

Food: Scheffer and Cottam (1935) examined the contents of 117 adult myna stomachs and found 39 percent animal and 61 percent vegetable matter. Animal matter included flies, moths and caterpillars, wasps, bees, ants, bugs, beetles, grasshoppers, spiders, and earthworms. Vegetable matter included wild varieties of elderberries, cherries, blueberries, crowberries, snowberries, salmonberries, loganberries, and serviceberries. Fruits of cultivated cherries, strawberries, raspberries, and blackberries were also eaten, with some damage done to apples, pears, cabbages, and lettuce.

88
Prothonotary warbler
Protonotaria citrea
L $4\frac{3}{4}''$

Habitat: The prothonotary warbler is found south of Canada in the eastern deciduous forests of the United States. Other names for this warbler (golden swamp warbler and willow warbler) describe its preference for swamps and periodically flooded areas. The prothonotary often lives near running water with streamside willows (Pearson 1936).

Nest: Nests are almost always in stumps and snags either standing in or near water (Simpson 1969) and often leaning over the water (Pearson 1936). Downy woodpecker and chickadee holes ranging from 2 to 12 feet and averaging 5 feet above the ground are used most often (Pearson 1936). However, the warbler reportedly has a wide tolerance for the type of nesting cavities used. Prothonotaries occasionally even nest in bird boxes and near buildings (Forbush and May 1939).

Food: Prothonotary warblers are primarily insectivorous. They eat ants, spiders, beetles, mayflies, and their larvae. They also will eat the larvae of water insects. This warbler feeds on trunks and branches of trees, shrubs, and fallen logs. They will also perch on rank grasses and water plants and eat small molluscs (Bent 1953).

89
Lucy's warbler
Vermivora luciae
L $4\frac{1}{4}''$

Habitat: This warbler inhabits mesquite woodlands and riparian vegetation with willows and cottonwoods from Nevada to the southwestern United States.

Nest: Nests of Lucy's warblers are usually located in tree cavities or under loose bark in willows, cottonwoods and mesquite. Ironwood, palo verde, and catclaw have also been used for nest trees (Robbins et al. 1966, Bent 1953, Peterson 1961).

Food: Insects are the major food items in the diet of Lucy's warbler (Bent 1953).

90
House sparrow
Passer domesticus
L 5¼″

Habitat: House sparrows are well known associates of man, thriving in towns and urban situations. They are also birds of the suburban-rural landscape (Summers-Smith 1963). Optimum habitat requirements are perhaps best met around buildings where waste grain from poultry and livestock feeding can be found. The species is scarce or absent from densely forested and desert regions uninhabited by man (Kalmbach 1940).

Nest: House sparrows nest in eaves, crevices, and holes in buildings; in vines and creepers on walls; in the branches of trees; in nest boxes and natural cavities in trees; and in other assorted locations, perhaps in that order of importance. Open tree nests may be built more often in warmer latitudes, but females seem to prefer hole nests (Cink 1976). Nesting cavities of cliff and bank swallows and house finches may be usurped. Nests are usually at least 6 to 8 feet from the ground, may be as high as 50 feet, and groups or colonies are not uncommon. Nests are domed whether in cavities or the open. House sparrows all too readily accept bird houses erected for purple martins, bluebirds, and other species.

Food: Kalmbach's (1940) study of the contents of 4,848 stomachs of suburban-rural birds indicated that adult and juvenile (non-nestling) house sparrows take 3.4 percent animal material throughout the year, particularly dung beetles, May beetles, and other Scarabaeidae. Grain from poultry yards, etc., made up the largest percentage of vegetable material (31.5 to 84.2 percent), followed by seeds of grasses and weeds (17 percent), and oats other than that in feed (14.4 percent). Ragweed, crabgrass, smartweed, and pigweed were important plants in the grass and weed category.

91
European tree sparrow
Passer montanus
L 5″

Habitat: The European tree sparrow was introduced in St. Louis, Missouri, in 1870. Coincident with the increase in house sparrows, European tree sparrows left the thickly settled parts of St. Louis and established populations throughout the city outskirts, suburban areas, farmyards, and woodlots. The species now occupies approximately 8,500 square miles in extreme east-central Missouri and west-central Illinois. They appear to be slowly expanding their range northward in western Illinois (Barlow 1973).

Nest: European tree sparrows nest in natural cavities, crevices, and woodpecker holes. They appear to be a weak competitor for available nesting sites. Part of the reason for the extension of tree sparrow range north may be related to large numbers of dead and dying American elms (victims of Dutch elm disease) which have provided an increasing source of nesting sites (Barlow 1973).

Food: Tree sparrows feed primarily on the ground on weed seeds, maize, insects, and spiders.

Literature Cited

Allen, Robert W., and Margaret M. Nice.
1952. A study of the breeding biology of the purple martin (Progne subis). Am. Midl. Nat. 47(3):606-665.

Bailey, Alfred M., and R. J. Niedrach.
1965. Birds of Colorado. Denver Mus. Nat. Hist., Denver, Colo. Vol. 1-2, 895 p.

Baker, W. Wilson.
1971. Observations on the food habits of the red-cockaded woodpecker. P. 100-107. In The ecology and management of the red-cockaded woodpecker: symposium proceedings, Okefenokee Natl. Wildl. Refuge, Folkston, Georgia, May 26-27, 1971. U.S. Dep. Int., Bur. Sport Fish. and Wildl. [Published in cooperation with Tall Timbers Res. Stn., Tallahassee, Florida.]

Baida, Russel P.
1975. The relationship of secondary cavity nesters to snag densities in western coniferous forests. U.S. For. Serv. Region 3, Albuquerque, New Mexico. Wildl. Habitat Tech. Bull. 1. 37 p.

Barlow, Jon C.
1973. Status of the North American population of the European tree sparrow. P. 10-23. In A symposium on the house sparrow (Passer domesticus) and European tree sparrow (P. montanus) in North America. AOU Ornithol. Monogr. 14.

Baumgartner, Luther L.
1939. Fox squirrel dens. J. Mammal. 20(4):456-465.

Beal, F. E. L.
1907. Birds of California in their relation to the fruit industry. Part I. Biol. Surv. Bull. 30.

Beal, F. E. L.
1911. Foods of the woodpeckers of the United States. U.S. Dep. Agric. Bull. 37. 64 p.

Beal, F. E. L., W. L. McAtee, and E. R. Kalmbach.
1916. Common birds of southeastern United States in relation to agriculture. U.S. Dep. Agric. Farmers' Bull. 755, p. 34-35.

Beal, F. E. L.
1918. Food habits of the swallows, a family of valuable native birds. U.S. Dep. Agric. Bull. 619. 28 p.

Beaver, Donald L.
1967. Feeding niches of flycatchers in a montane forest in Colorado. M.S. Thesis. Colorado State Univ. 122 p.

Beckett, Ted.
1971. A summary of red-cockaded woodpecker observations in South Carolina. P. 87-95. In The ecology and management of the red-cockaded woodpecker: symposium

proceedings, Okefenokee Natl. Wildl. Refuge, Folkston, Georgia, May 26-27, 1971. U.S. Dept. Int., Bur. Sport Fish. Wildl., [Published in cooperation with Tall Timbers Res. Stn., Tallahassee, Florida.]

Bellrose, Frank C., Kenneth L. Johnson and T. Udell Meyers.
1964. Relative value of natural cavities and nesting houses for wood ducks. J. Wildl. Manage. 28(4):661-676.

Bellrose, Frank C.
1976. Ducks, geese and swans of North America. Stackpole Books, Harrisburg, PA. 543 p.

Bellrose, Frank, Jr.
1938. Duck hawks nesting in western Tennessee. Wilson Bull. 50(2):139.

Bendire, Charles E.
1892. Life histories of North American birds. U.S. Natl. Mus. Spec. Bull. 1.

Bent, Arthur C.
1923. Life histories of North American waterfowl. Part I. U.S. Natl. Mus. Bull. 126, Wash., D.C. 244 p. (Reprinted by Dover Publ., Inc., New York 1962).

Bent, Arthur C.
1937. Life histories of North American birds of prey. Vol. I. U.S. Natl. Mus. Bull. 167, Wash., D.C. 409 p. (Reprinted by Dover Publ., Inc., New York 1961).

Bent, Arthur C.
1938. Life histories of North American birds of prey. Vol. II. U.S. Natl. Mus. Bull. 170, Wash., D.C. 495 p. (Reprinted by Dover Publ., Inc., New York 1961).

Bent, Arthur C.
1939. Life histories of North American woodpeckers. U.S. Natl. Mus. Bull. 174, Wash., D.C. 334 p. (Reprinted by Dover Publ., Inc., New York 1964).

Bent, Arthur C.
1940. Life histories of North American cuckoos, goatsuckers, hummingbirds, and their allies. U.S. Natl. Mus. Bull. 176, Wash., D.C. 506 p. (Reprinted by Dover Publ., Inc., New York 1964).

Bent, Arthur C.
1942. Life histories of North American flycatchers, larks, swallows, and their allies. U.S. Natl. Mus. Bull. 179, Wash., D.C. 555 p. (Reprinted by Dover Publ., Inc., New York 1963).

Bent, Arthur C.
1946. Life histories of North American jays, crows, and titmice. U.S. Natl. Mus. Bull. 191, Wash., D.C. 495 p. (Reprinted by Dover Publ., Inc., New York 1964).

Bent, Arthur C.
1948. Life histories of North American nuthatches, wrens, thrashers, and their allies. U.S. Natl. Mus. Bull. 195, Wash., D.C. 475 p. (Reprinted by Dover Publ., Inc., New York 1964).

Bent, Arthur C.
1949. Life histories of North American thrushes, kinglets, and their allies. U.S. Natl. Mus. Bull. 196, Wash., D.C. 454 p.

Bent, Arthur C.
1950. Life histories of North American wagtails, shrikes, vireos, and their allies. U.S. Natl. Mus. Bull. 197, Wash., D.C. 411 p. (Reprinted by Dover Publ., Inc., New York 1965).

Bent, Arthur C.
1953. Life histories of North American wood warblers. U.S. Natl. Mus. Bull. 203, Wash., D.C. 734 p.

Bock, Carl F.
1970. The ecology and behavior of the Lewis woodpecker (Asyndesmus lewis). Univ. Calif. Publ. Zoology, Vol. 92, 100 p. Univ. Calif. Press, Berkeley and Los Angeles.

Bolen, E. G.
1967. Nesting boxes for black-bellied tree ducks. J. Wildl. Manage. 31(4):794-797.

Bolen, Eric G. and Billy J. Forsyth.
1967. Foods of the black-bellied tree duck in south Texas. Wilson Bull. 79(1):43-49.

Bolen, E. G., B. McDaniel, and C. Cottam.
1964. Natural history of the black-bellied tree duck (Dendrocygna autumnalis) in southern Texas. Southwest Nat. 9(2):78-88.

Brewer, Richard.
1961. Comparative notes on the life history of the Carolina chickadee. Wilson Bull. 73(4):348-373.

Brock, Elbert M.
1958. Some prey of the pygmy owl. Condor 60(5):338.

Brown, Leslie, and Dean Amadon.
1968. Falco peregrinus, peregrine falcon. P. 850-856. In Eagles, hawks and falcons of the world. Vol. 2. McGraw-Hill, New York.

Brown, Vinson, and Henry G. Weston, Jr.
1961. Handbook of California Birds. Naturegraph Co., Calif. 224 p.

Bruns, Herbert.
1960. The economic importance of birds in forests. Bird Study 7(4):193-208.

Bunch, Carl H.
1964. Nesting of the western purple martin. Murrelet 45(1):10-11.

Burleigh, Thomas D.
1972. Birds of Idaho. The Caxtonprinters Ld., Caldwell, Idaho. 467 p.

Burton, J. A., ed.
1973. Owls of the world. E. P. Dalton and Co., Inc., New York. 216 p.

95

Carter, Brian C.
1958. The American goldeneye in central New Brunswick. Canadian Wildl. Serv. Wildl. Manage. Bull., Series 2(9). 47 p.

Catling, Paul M.
1972. A study of the boreal owl in southern Ontario with particular reference to the irruption of 1968-69. Can. Field Nat. 86(3):223-232.

Cink, C. L.
1976. The influence of early learning on nest site selection in the house sparrow. Condor 78(1):103-104.

Conner, Richard N., Robert G. Hooper, Hewlette S. Crawford, and Henry S. Mosby.
1975. Woodpecker nesting habitat in cut and uncut woodlands in Virginia. J. Wildl. Manage. 39(1):144-150.

Cooke, W. W.
1888. Report on bird migration in the Mississippi Valley in the years 1884 and 1885. U.S. Dep. Agric., Div. Econ. Ornith., Bull. 2. 313 p.

Cottam, Clarence.

1939. Food habits of North American diving ducks. U.S. Dep. Agric. Tech. Bull. 643. 140 p.

Craighead, John, and Frank Craighead.
1940. Nesting pigeon hawks. Wilson Bull. 52:241-248.

Crockett, Allen B., and Harlow H. Hadow.
1975. Nest site selection by Williamson and red-naped sapsuckers. Condor 77(3):365-368.

Crosby, Gilbert T.
1971. Ecology of the red-cockaded woodpecker in the nesting season. M.S. thesis. Univ. of Florida, Gainesville.

Davis, John, George F. Fisher, and Betty S. Davis.
1963. The breeding biology of the western flycatcher. Condor 65(5):337-382.

de Kiriline, Louise.
1952. Red-breast makes a home. Audubon 54(1):16-21.

Dennis, John V.
1967. The ivory-bill flies still. Audubon 11:38-45.

Dippie, George F.
1895. Nesting of Richardson's merlin. Oologist 11:236-237.

Dunn, Harry H.
1901. The spotted owl. Oologist 18:165-167.

Emlen, John T., Jr.
1937. Bird damage to almonds in California. Condor 39:192-197.

Erskine, Anthony J.
1971. Buffleheads. Canadian Wildl. Serv., Monograph Series 4. 240 pp.

Erskine, A. J., and W. D. McLaren.
1972. Sapsucker nest holes and their use by other species. Can. Field. Nat. 86(4):357-361.

96

Ferguson, Henry L.
1922. The fall migration of hawks as observed at Fisher's Island, New York. Auk 18:488-496.

Fisher, Albert K.
1893. The hawks and owls of the United States and their relations to agriculture. Bull. 3. 210 p. U.S. Govt. Print. Off., Wash., D.C.

Forbush, Edward Howe, and John Bichard May.
1939. A natural history of American birds of eastern and central North America. Bramhall House, New York. 552 p.

Foreman, Larry D.
1976. Nest site and activity of an incubating common merganser in northwestern California. Calif. Fish and Game 62(1):87-88.

Forsman, Eric.
1976. The spotted owl in Oregon. M.S. Thesis. Oregon State Univ. 131 p.

Fyfe, Richard.
1969. The peregrine falcon in the Canadian arctic and eastern North America. In J. J. Hickey, ed. Peregrine Falcon Populations. Univ. of Wisconsin Press. Milwaukee.

Ganier, A. F.
1932. Duck Hawk at Reelfoot Herony. Migrant 3(2):28-32.

Gibbs, Richard M.

1961. Breeding ecology of the common goldeneye, Bucephala clangula americana, in Maine. M.S. Thesis. Univ. Maine, Orono. 113 p.

Gibo, D. L., R. Stephens, A. Culpeper, and H. Dew.

1976. Nest site preferences and nesting success of the starling, Sturnus vulgaris L., in marginal and favorable habitats in Mississauga, Ontario, Canada. Am. Midl. Nat. 95(2):493-499.

Gillespie, Mabel.

1930. Behavior and local distribution of tufted titmice in winter and spring. Bird-Banding 1(3):113-127.

Gingrich, William F.

1914. Young turkey vultures. Bird Lore 16(4):281.

Givens, Lawrence S.

1971. Introduction to the symposium on the ecology and management of the red-cockaded woodpecker. P. 1-3. In The ecology and management of the red-cockaded woodpecker: Symposium Proceedings, Okefenokee Natl. Wildl. Refuge, Folkston, Georgia, May 26-27, 1971. U.S. Dept. Int., Bur. Sport Fish. Wildl. [Published in cooperation with Tall Timbers Res. Stn., Tallahassee, Florida.]

Godfrey, W. Earl.

1966. The birds of Canada. Natl. Mus. Can. Bull. 203. Ottawa, Ontario. 428 p.

Goss, Nathaniel S.

1878. Breeding of the duck hawk in trees. Nutt. Ornithol. Club Bull. 3:32-34.

97

Greenway, James C., Jr.

1958. Extinct and vanishing birds of the world. Am. Comm, for Int. Wildl. Protection Spec. Publ. No. 13. p. 357-362.

Grenquist, P.

1965. Changes in abundance of some duck and seabird populations of the coast of Finland 1949-1963. Finn. Game Res. 27:1-114.

Grice, David, and John P. Rogers.

1965. The wood duck in Massachusetts. Final rep. Fed. Aid in Wildl. Restor. Proj. W-19-R. 96 p.

Grinnell, Joseph, and Tracy Storer.

1924. Animal life in the Yosemite. Univ. of Calif. Press, Berkeley, 752 p.

Grinnell, Joseph, and Alden H. Miller.

1944. The distribution of the birds of California. Cooper Ornithol. Club. 27. 608 p.

Gysel, Leslie W.

1961. An ecological study of tree cavities and ground burrows in forest stands. J. Wildl. Manage. 25(1):12-20.

Hadow, Harlow H.

1973. Winter ecology of migrant and resident Lewis' woodpeckers in southeastern Colorado. Condor 75(2):210-224.

Hamerstrom, Frances.

1972. Birds of prey of Wisconsin. Dep. Nat. Res., Madison, Wis. 64 p.

Hamerstrom, Frances, Frederick N. Hamerstrom, and John Hart.

1973. Nest boxes: an effective management tool for kestrels. J. Wildl. Manage. 37(3):400-403.

Hansen, Henry L.

1966. Silvical characteristics of tree species and decay processes as related to cavity production. P. 65-69. In L. R. Jahn (ed.,) Wood duck management and research: a symposium. Wildl. Manage. Inst. Wash., D.C. 212 p.

Harris, Stanley W., Charles L. Buechele, and Charles F. Yocum.
1954. The status of Barrow's golden-eye in eastern Washington. Murrelet 35(3):33-38.

Hayes, Allan, and Pauline James.
1963. Elf owl rediscovered in lower Rio Grande delta of Texas. Wilson Bull. 75:179-182.

Henderson, Archibald D.
1919. Nesting of the American hawk owl. Oologist 36:59-63.

Henderson, Archibald D.
1925. With the early breeders. Oologist 40:126-127.

Hespenheide, Henry A.
1971. Flycatcher habitat selection in the eastern deciduous forest. Auk 88(1):61-74.

Hickey, Joseph J.
1942. Eastern populations of the duck hawk. Auk 59(2):176-204.

Hickey, Joseph J., and Daniel W. Anderson.
1969. The peregrine falcon: life history and population literature. P. 3-42. In J. J. Hickey, ed. Peregrine falcon populations. Univ. of Wisconsin Press, Milwaukee.

Hopkins, Melvin L., and Teddy E. Lynn, Jr.
1971. Some characteristics of the red-cockaded woodpecker cavity trees and management implications in South Carolina. P. 140-169. In The ecology and management of the red-cockaded woodpecker; symposium proceedings, Okefenokee Natl. Wildl. Refuge, Folkston, Georgia, May 26-27, 1971. U.S. Dep. Int., Bur. Sport Fish. Wildl. [Published in cooperation with Tall Timbers Res. Stn., Tallahassee, Florida.]

Houseman, J. E.
1894. Nesting habits of Richardson's merlin. Oologist 11:236-237.

Howell, Thomas R.
1952. Natural history and differentiation in the yellow-bellied sapsucker. Condor 54(5):237-282.

Hoxie, Walter J.
1886. Breeding habits of the black vulture. Auk 3(2):245-247.

Hoyt, J. Southgate Y.
1941. Through the year with the pileated woodpecker. Audubon 43(6):525-528.

Hoyt, Sally F.
1957. The ecology of the pileated woodpecker. Ecology 38(2):246-256.

Hubbard, John P.
1965. Summer birds of the Mogollon Mountains, New Mexico. Condor 67:404-415.

Huey, Lawrence M.
1932. Note on the food of an Arizona spotted owl. Condor 34:100-101.

Jackman, Siri M.
1975. Woodpeckers in the Pacific northwest in relation to the forest and its inhabitants. M.S. Thesis. Oregon State Univ. 147 p.

Jackman, Siri M., and J. Michael Scott.
1975. Literature review of twenty-three selected forest birds of the Pacific northwest. U.S. For. Serv., Region 6. p. 339-353.

Jackson, Jerome A.

1971. The evolution, taxonomy, distribution, past populations, and current status of the red-cockaded woodpecker. P. 4-29. In The ecology and management of the red-cockaded woodpecker: symposium proceedings, Okefenokee Natl. Wildl. Refuge, Folkston, Georgia, May 26-27, 1971. U.S. Dep. Int., Bur. Sport Fish. Wildl. [Published in cooperation with Tall Timbers Res. Stn., Tallahassee, Florida.]

99

Jackson, Thomas.
1903. The turkey vulture and its young. Bird Lore 5(6):184-187.

Jacot, Edouard C.
1931. Notes on the spotted and flammulated screech owls in Arizona. Condor 33(1):8-11.

Johnsgard, Paul A.
1975. Waterfowl of North America. Indiana Univ. Press, Bloomington. 575 p.

Johnson, Leon L.
1967. The common goldeneye duck and the role of nesting boxes in its management in north-central Minnesota. J. Minnesota Acad. Sci. 34:110-113.

Johnston, Richard F.
1967. Seasonal variations in the food of the purple martin Progne subis in Kansas. Ibis 109(1):8-13.

Kale, Herbert W.
1968. The relationship of purple martins to mosquito control. Auk 85(4):651-661.

Kalmbach, E. R.
1928. The European starling in the United States. U.S. Dep. Agric. Farmers' Bull. 1571. 27 p.

Kalmbach, E. R.
1940. Economic status of the English sparrow in the United States. U.S. Dep. Agric. Tech. Bull. 711. 66 p.

Karalus, Karl E., and Allan W. Eckert.
1974. The owls of North America. Doubleday & Co., Inc., New York. 278 p.

Kempton, Russell Marshall.
1927. Notes on the home life of the turkey vulture. Wilson Bull. 39(3):142-145.

Kenyon, Karl W.
1947. Cause of death of a flammulated owl. Condor 49:88.

Kessel, Brina.
1957. A study of the breeding biology of the European starling (Sturnus vulgaris L.) in North America. Am. Midl. Nat. 58(2):257-331.

Kilham, Lawrence.
1958. Pair formation, mutual tapping, and nest hole selection of red-bellied woodpeckers. Auk 75(3):318-329.

Kilham, Lawrence.
1962. Reproductive behavior of downy woodpeckers. Condor 64(2):126-133.

Kilham, Lawrence.
1963. Food storing of red-bellied woodpeckers. Wilson Bull. 75(3):227-234.

Kilham, Lawrence.
1968a. Reproductive behavior of hairy woodpeckers. H. Nesting and habitat. Wilson Bull. 80(3):286-305.

Kilham, Lawrence.
1968b. Reproductive behavior of white-breasted nuthatches. I. Distraction display, bill-sweeping, and nest-hole defense. Auk 85(3):477-492.

Kilham, Lawrence.
1970. Feeding behavior of downy woodpeckers. I. Preference for paper birches and sexual differences. Auk 87(3):544-556.

Kilham, Lawrence
1971. Reproductive behavior of yellow-bellied sapsuckers. I. Preference for nesting in Fomes infected aspens, and nest hole interrelationships with flying squirrels, raccoons, and other animals. Wilson Bull. 83:159-171.

Koplin, James R.
1972. Measuring predator impact of woodpeckers on spruce beetles. J. Wildl. Manage. 36(2):308-320.

Korschgen, Leroy J., and Henry S. Stuart.
1972. Twenty years of avian predator-small mammal relationships in Missouri. J. Wildl. Manage. 36(2):269-282.

Laskey, Amelia R.
1940. The 1939 nesting season of bluebirds at Nashville, Tennessee. Wilson Bull. 52:183-190.

Laskey, Amelia R.
1948. Some nesting data on the Carolina wren at Nashville, Tennessee. Bird-Banding 19(3):101-121.

Laskey, Amelia R.
1957. Some tufted titmouse life history. Bird-Banding 28(3):135-145.

Lawrence, Alexander G.
1932. New Manitoba nesting records. Free Press Evening Bull., Winnipeg. 27 May.

Lawrence, Louise de K.
1949. Notes on nesting pigeon hawks at Pimisi Bay, Ontario. Wilson Bull. 61:15-25.

Lawrence, Louise de K.
1967. A comparative life history of four species of woodpeckers. Ornithol. Monogr. 5:1-156.

Ligon, J. David.
1967. The biology of the elf owl, Micrathene whitneyi. Ph.D. Diss. Michigan Univ.

Ligon, J. David.
1971. Some factors influencing numbers of the red-cockaded woodpecker. P. 30-43. In The ecology and management of the red-cockaded woodpecker: symposium proceedings, Okefenokee Natl. Wildl. Refuge, Folkston, Georgia, May 26-27, 1971. U.S. Dep. Int., Bur. Sport Fish. Wildl. [Published in cooperation with Tall Timbers Res. Stn., Tallahassee, Florida.]

Ligon, J. David.
1973. Foraging behavior of the white-headed woodpecker in Idaho. Auk 90(4):862-869.

Ligon, J. Stokley.
1961. New Mexico birds and where to find them. Univ. of New Mexico Press, Albuquerque. 360 p.

Low, Seth H.
1933. Further notes on nesting of the tree swallows. Bird-Banding 4(2):76-87.

Lowry, George Hines, Jr.
1960. Louisiana birds. Louisiana State Univ. Press, Baton Rouge.

Mackay, Violet M., and William M. Hughes.

1963. Crested mynah in British Columbia. Can. Field Nat. 77(3):154-162.

MacLellan, C. R.
1958. Role of woodpeckers in control of the codling moth in Nova Scotia. Can. Entomol. 90(1):18-22.

MacLellan, C. R.
1959. Woodpeckers as predators of the codling moth in Nova Scotia. Can. Entomol. 91(11):673-680.

MacRoberts, Barbara R., and M. H. MacRoberts.
1972. A most social bird. Nat. Hist. 81(10):44-51.

Marshall, Joe T.
1942. Food and habitat of the spotted owl. Condor 44:66-67.

Marti, Carl D.
1974. Feeding ecology of four sympatric owls. Condor 76(1):45-61.

Martin, Alexander C., Herbert S. Zim, and Arnold L. Nelson.
1951. American wildlife and plants. McGraw-Hill Book Co. Inc., New York. 500 p.

Massey, Calvin L., and Noel D. Wygant.
1973. Woodpeckers: most important predator of the spruce beetle. Colo. Field Ornithol. 16:4-8.

McAtee, W. L.
1911. Woodpeckers in relation to trees and wood products. U.S. Dep. Agric. Biol. Surv. Bull. 39.

McClelland, B. Riley, and Sidney S. Frissell.
1975. Identifying forest snags useful for hole-nesting birds. J. For. 73(7):414-418.

McGilvrey, Frank B. (Compiler).
1968. A guide to wood duck production habitat requirements. U.S. Bur. Sport Fish, and Wildl., Resource Pub. 60. 32 p.

McLaren, Margaret A.
1975. Breeding biology of the boreal chickadee. Wilson Bull. 87(3):344-354.

Meanley, Brooke, and Ann Gilkeson Meanley.
1958. Nesting habitat of the black-bellied tree duck in Texas. Wilson Bull. 70(1):94-95.

Mendall, H. L.
1944. Food of hawks and owls in Maine. J. Wildl. Manage. 8:198-208.

Miller, Alden H., and Carl E. Bock.
1972. Natural history of the Nuttall woodpecker at Hastings Reservation. Condor 74(3):284-294.

102

Miller, Edwin V.
1941. Behavior of the Bewick wren. Condor 43(2):81-99.

Morse, Thomas E., Joel L. Jakabosky, and Vernon P. McCrow.
1969. Some aspects of the breeding biology of the hooded merganser. J. Wildl. Manage. 33(3):596-604.

Nelson, Morlan W.
1969. The status of the peregrine falcon in the northwest. P. 61-72. In J. J. Hickey, ed. Peregrine falcon populations. Univ. of Wisconsin Press, Milwaukee.

Nice, Margaret M., and Ruth H. Thomas.
1948. A nesting of the Carolina wren. Wilson Bull. 60(3):139-158.

Nicholls, Thomas H., and Dwain W. Warner.

1972. Barred owl habitat use as determined by radiotelemetry. J. Wildl. Manage. 36(2):213-224.

Oberholser, Harry C.
1974. The bird life of Texas. Vol. 1. Univ. of Texas Press, Austin. 530 p.

Odum, Eugene P.
1941. Annual cycle of the black-capped chickadee—1. Auk 58(3):314-333.

Odum, Eugene P.
1942. Annual cycle of the black-capped chickadee—3. Auk 59(4):499-531.

Oliver, William W.
1970. The feeding patterns of sapsuckers on ponderosa pine in northeastern California. Condor 72(2):241.

Olson, Harold.
1953. Beetle rout in the Rockies. Audubon 55(1):30-32.

Packard, Fred Mallery.
1945. Birds of Rocky Mountain National Park. Auk 62(3):371-394.

Palmer, Ralph S. (ed.)
1976. Handbook of North American birds. Vol. 3. Yale Univ. Press, New Haven, Conn. 560 p.

Pearson, T. Gilbert (ed.)
1936. Birds of America. Garden City Books, Garden City, New York. 289 p.

Peterson, Roger Tory.
1948. Birds over America. Dodd, Mead, and Co., New York. 342 p.

Peterson, Roger Tory.
1961. A field guide to western birds. Houghton Mifflin Co., Boston. 309 p.

Phillips, Allan, Joe Marshall, and Gale Monson.
1964. The birds of Arizona. Univ. of Ariz. Press, Tucson. 212 p.

Planck, Roy J.
1967. Nest site selection and nesting of the European starling (Sturnus vulgaris L.) in California. Ph.D. Thesis, Univ. Calif., Davis. 111 p.

103

Pough, Richard H.
1957. Audubon western bird guide. Doubleday and Co. Inc., Garden City, New York. 316 p.

Preble, Edward A.
1908. A biological investigation of the Athabaska-Mackenzie region. N. Am. Fauna 27.

Prince, Harold H.
1968. Nest sites used by wood ducks and common golden-eyes in New Brunswick. J. Wildl. Manage. 32(3):489-500.

Rasmussen, D. Irvin.
1941. Biotic communities of the Kaibab Plateau, Arizona. Ecol. Monogr. 11(3):229-275.

Reed, Chester A.
1965. North American bird eggs. Dover Publications Inc., New York. 372 p.

Reed, J. Harris.
1897. Notes on the American barn owl in eastern Pennsylvania. Auk 14(4):374-383.

Reller, Ann Willbern.
1972. Aspects of behavioral ecology of red-headed and red-bellied woodpeckers. Am. Midl. Nat. 88(2):270-290.

Ridgway, Robert.
1889. The Ornithology of Illinois. Vol. 1. Plantagraph Printing & Stationery Co., Bloomington, Ill. 550 p.
Robbins, Chandler S., Bertel Bruun, and Herbert S. Zim.
1966. Birds of North America. Golden Press, New York. 340 p.
Roest, A. I.
1957. Notes on the American sparrow hawk. Auk 74(1):1-19.
Royall, Willis C., Jr.
1966. Breeding of the starling in central Arizona. Condor 68(2):196-205.
Rustad, Orwin A.
1972. An eastern bluebird nesting study in south central Minnesota. Loon 44(3):80-84.
Rylander, Michael Kent and Eric G. Bolen.
1974. Feeding adaptations in whistling ducks (Dendrocygna). Auk 91(1):86-94.
Scheffer, T. H., and C. Cottam.
1935. The crested myna, or Chinese starling, in the Pacific northwest. U.S. Dep. Agric. Tech. Bull. 467.
Scott, Virgil E., and David R. Patton.
1975. Cavity-nesting birds of Arizona and New Mexico forests. USDA. For. Serv. Gen. Tech. Rep. RM-10, Rocky Mt. For. and Range Exp. Stn., Fort Collins, CO 52 p.
Short, Lester L.
1971. Systematics and behavior of some North American woodpeckers, genus Picoides. Am. Mus. Nat. Hist. Bull. 145(1):1-118.
Simpson, Marcus B., Jr.
1969. The prothonotary warbler in the Carolina Piedmont. Chat 33(2):31-37.
104
Small, Arnold.
1974. The birds of California. Winchester Press, New York. 310 p.
Spofford, W. R.
1942. Nesting of the peregrine falcon in Tennessee. Migrant 13(2):29-31.
Spofford, W. R.
1943. Peregrines in a western Tennessee swamp. Migrant 14:25.
Spofford, W. R.
1945. Peregrine falcons in a western Tennessee swamp. Migrant 16:50-58.
Spofford, W. R.
1947. Another tree nesting peregrine falcon record for Tennessee. Migrant 18(4):60.
Sprunt, Alexander, and E. Burnham Chamberlain.
1949. South Carolina bird life. Univ. South Carolina Press, Columbia. 655 p.
Strange, Thomas H., Earl R. Cunningham, and John W. Goertz.
1971. Use of nest boxes by wood ducks in Mississippi. J. Wildl. Manage. 35(4):786-793.
Summers-Smith, D.
1963. The house sparrow. New Nat. Ser. Spec. Vol., St. James Place, London, England. 269 p.
Sutton, George Miksch.
1930. The nesting wrens of Brooks County, West Virginia. Wilson Bull. 42(1):10-17.
Sutton, George Miksch.
1967. Oklahoma birds. Univ. Oklahoma Press, Norman. 674 p.
Tanner, J. T.

1942. The Ivory-billed woodpecker. Nat. Audubon Soc. Res. Rep. 1.

Tate, James, Jr.

1973. Methods and annual sequence of foraging by the sapsucker. Auk 90(4):840-855.

Tatschl, John L.

1967. Breeding birds of the Sandia Mountains and their ecological distribution. Condor 69(5):479-490.

Telford, Allan D., and G. G. Herman.

1963. Chickadee helps check insect invasion. Audubon Mag. 65(2):78-81.

Tevis, Lloyd, Jr.

1953. Effect of vertebrate animals on seed crop of sugar pine. J. Wildl. Manage. 17(2):128-131.

Thomas, Jack Ward, Glenn L. Crouch, Roger S. Bumstead, and Larry D. Bryant.

1975. Silvicultural options and habitat values in coniferous forests. P. 272-287. In Proc. Symp. on Manage. For. and Range Habits for Non-game Birds. Dixie R. Smith. Tech. Coord. USDA For. Serv. Gen. Tech. Rep. WO-1. Wash., D.C. 343 p.

Thomas, Jack Ward, Rodney J. Miller, Hugh Black, Jon E. Rodiek, and Chris Maser.

1976. Guidelines for maintaining and enhancing wildlife habitat in forest management in the Blue Mountains of Oregon and Washington. 41st N. Am. Wildl. and Nat. Resour. Conf., Wash., D.C. 45 p.

Thomas, Ruth Harris.

1946. A study of eastern bluebirds in Arkansas. Wilson Bull. 58(3):143-183.

Townsend, Manley Bacon.

1914. Turkey vultures in northwestern Iowa. Bird Lore 16(4):279-280.

Troetschler, Ruth G.

1976. Acorn woodpecker breeding strategy as affected by starling nest-hole competition. Condor 78(2):151-165.

Tufts, Robie W.

1925. Nesting of the Richardson's owl. Can. Field Nat. 39:85-86.

U.S. Department of Agriculture, Forest Service.

1976. For. Serv. Manual—Title 5100—Fire Management. R-3 Suppl. 119:5151.13b-5152.23d.

U.S. Department of Agriculture, Forest Service.

1977. For. Serv. Manual—Title 2630.3 (Policy)—Wildlife Management.

U.S. Fish and Wildlife Service.

1976. Nest boxes for wood ducks. Wildl. Leafl. 510. 16 p. (unnumbered).

von Haartman, Lars.

1956. Territory in the pied flycatcher. Ibis 98(3):461-475.

von Haartman, Lars.

1968. The evolution of resident versus migratory habits in birds: some considerations. Ornis Fenn. 45(1):1-7.

Ward, Billy.

1930. Red-cockaded woodpeckers on corn. Bird Lore 32(2):127-128.

West, J. David, and J. Murray Speiers.

1959. The 1956-1957 invasion of three-toed woodpeckers. Wilson Bull. 71(4):348-363.

Wetmore, Alexander.

1964. Song and garden birds of North America. Nat. Geogr. Soc., Wash., D.C. 400 p.

White, Clayton M., and David G. Roseneau.
1970. Observations on food, nesting, and winter populations of large North American falcons. Condor 72(1):113-115.

Whittle, Charles L.
1926. Notes on the nesting habits of tree swallows. Auk 43(2):247-248.

Winternitz, Barbara L.
1973. Ecological patterns in a montane breeding bird community. Ph.D. Diss., Univ. of Colo. 106

Plants Referred to in Text:

Common Name	Scientific Name
Agave	Agave sp.
Alder	Alnus sp.
Almond	Prunus sp.
American linden	Tilia americana L.
Anaqua	Ehretia anacua (Teran & Berl.) I. M. Johnst.
Apple	Malus sp.
Arrow arum	Peltandra sp.
Ash	Fraxinus sp.
Ash, black	Fraxinus nigra Marsh.
Ash, green	Fraxinus pennsylvanica Marsh.
Ash, water	Fraxinus caroliniana Mill.
Aspen	Populus sp.
Baldcypress	Taxodium distichum (L.) Rich.
Basswood	Tilia sp.
Bayberry	Myrica sp.
Beech	Fagus grandifolia Ehrh.
Bermuda grass	Cynodom dactylon (L.) Pers.
Birch	Betula sp.
Birch, paper	Betula papyrifera Marsh.
Blackberries	Rubus sp.
Blueberries	Vaccinium sp.
Bulrush	Scirpus sp.
Butternut	Juglans cinerea L.
Buttonbush	Cephalanthus occidentalis L.
Cabbage	Brassica sp.
Cactus	Cactaceae
Catalpa	Catalpa sp.
Catclaw	Acacia sp.
Cedar	
Cherries	Prunus sp.
Cherry, wild	Prunus sp.
China tree	Koelreuteria sp.
Cissus	Cissus sp.
Coontail	Ceratophyllum demersum L.
Corn	Zea mays L.
Cottonwood	Populus sp.

Common name	Scientific name
Cottonwood, black	Populus trichocarpa Torr. & Gray
Crabgrass	Digitaria sp.
Creosote bush	Larrea tridentata (DC.) Cov.
Crowberries	Empetrum sp.
Currant	Ribes sp.
Cypress	
Dogwood	Cornus sp.
Douglas-fir	Pseudotsuga menziesii (Mirb.) Franco
Duckweed	Lemna sp.
Ebony	Diospyros sp.
Elderberry	Sambucus sp.
Elm	Ulmus sp.
Elm, American	Ulmus americana L.
Fig	Ficus sp.
Fir	Abies sp.
Fir, balsam	Abies balsamea (L.) Mill.
Fir, red	Abies magnifica A. Murr.
Fir, subalpine	Abies lasiocarpa (Hook.) Nutt.
Fir, white	Abies concolor (Gord. & Glend.) Lindl.
Grapes, wild	Vitis sp.
Gum, black	Nyssa sylvatica Marsh.
Gum, sour	Nyssa sp.
Hackberry	Celtis sp.
Hazelnut	Corylus sp.
Hemlock	Tsuga sp.
Hickory	Carya sp.
Hickory, bitternut	Carya cordiformis (Wangenh.) K. Koch
Holly	Ilex sp.
Honeysuckle	Lonicera sp.
Huisache	Acacia farnesiana (L.) Willd.
Ironwood	Olneya tesota Gray
Juniper	Juniperus sp.
Larch	Larix sp.
Larch, western	Larix occidentalis Nutt.
Lettuce	Lactuca sp.
Loganberries	Rubus sp.
Magnolia	Magnolia sp.
Maize	Zea mays L.
Maple	Acer sp.
Maple, red	Acer rubrum L.
Maple, silver	Acer saccharinum L.
Mescal	Agave sp.
Mesquite	Prosopis sp.
Millet	Setaria sp.
Mistletoe	Phoradendron sp.
Oak	Quercus sp.
Oak, black	Quercus velutina Lam.
Oak, blackjack	Q. marilandica Muenchh.
Oak, bur	Q. macrocarpa Michx.

Oak, cherrybark	Q. falcata var. pagodaefolia Ell.
Oak, live	Q. virginiana Mill.
Oak, overcup	Q. lyrata Walt.
Oak, pin	Q. palustris Muenchh.
Oak, red	Quercus sp.
Oak, white	Q. alba L.
Oats	Avena sp.
Palmetto	Sabal sp.
Palo Verde	Cercidium sp.
Pear	Pyrus sp.
Pecan	Carya illinoensis (Wang.) K. Koch
Pepper, red	Capsicum sp.
Pigweed	Chenopodium sp.
Pine	Pinus sp.
Pine, Bishop	Pinus muricata D. Don.
Pine, Jeffrey	P. jeffreyi Grev. & Balf.
Pine, loblolly	P. taeda L.
Pine, lodgepole	P. contorta Dougl.
Pine, longleaf	P. palustris Mill.
Pine, Monterey	P. radiata D. Don.
Pine, pinyon	P. edulis Engelm.
Pine, ponderosa	P. ponderosa Laws.
Pine, shortleaf	P. echinata Mill.
Pine, slash	P. elliotti Engelm.
Pine, sugar	P. lambertiana Dougl.
Pine, white	P. strobus L.
Poison ivy	Rhus radicans L.
Poison oak	Rhus diversiloba T. & G.
Pokeberry	Phytolacca americana L.
Pondweed	Potamogeton sp.
Poplar	Populus sp.
Poplar, balsam	Populus balsamifera L.
Prunes	Prunus sp.
Ragweed	Ambrosia sp.
Raspberries	Rubus sp.
Red heart fungus	Fomes sp.
Redwood	Sequoia sempervirens (D. Don.) Endl.
Retama	Retama sp.
Sago pondweed	Potamogeton pectinatus L.
Saguaro cactus	Carnegiea gigantea (Engelm.) Britt. & Rose
Salmonberries	Rubus spectabilis Pursh.
Sawgrass, tall	Cladium sp.
Screwbean	Prosopis sp.
Serviceberries	Amelanchier sp.
Skunk cabbage	Symplocarpus foetidus (L.) Nutt.
Smartweed	Polygonum sp.
Snowberries	Symphoricarpos sp.
Sorghum	Sorghum sp.
Spruce	Picea sp.

Spruce, Engelmann   Picea engelmannii Parry
Spruce, Sitka Picea sitchensis (Bong.) Carr.
Strawberries Fragraria sp.
Sumac   Rhus sp.
Sunflower   Helianthus sp.
Sweetgum   Liquidambar styraciflua L.
Sycamore   Platanus sp.
Tamarac   Larix laricina (Du Roi) K. Koch
Tulip-poplar Liriodendron tulipifera L.
Tupelo   Nyssa sylvatica Marsh.
Virginia creeper   Parthenocissus quinquefolia L.
Walnut   Juglans sp.
Water stargrass   Heteranthera dubia (Jacq.) MacM.
Wax-myrtle   Myrica cerifera L.
Wheat   Triticum sp.
Widegon grass   Ruppia maritima L.
Wild celery Vallisneria americana Michx.
Willow   Salix sp.
Willow, black   Salix nigra Marsh.
Yucca   Yucca sp.
110
Invertebrates Referred to in Text:
Common Name   Class or Order   Family   Genus and Species
Amphipods Crustacea
Ants   Hymenoptera   Formicidae
Aphids   Homoptera   Aphididae
Assassin bugs   Hemiptera   Reduviidae
Bark beetles Coleoptera   Scolytidae
Bees   Hymenoptera   Apidae
Beetles   Coleoptera
Black crickets   Orthoptera   Gryllidae
Blue mussel (phylum) Mollusca
Boll weevil Coleoptera   Curculionidae   Anthonomus grandis Boheman
Bugs   Hemiptera
Butterflies Lepidoptera
Caddis flies Trichoptera
Carpenter ants   Hymenoptera   Formicidae   Camponotus sp.
Caterpillars Lepidoptera
Centipedes   Chilopoda
Chironomids   Diptera   Chironomidae
Cicadas   Homoptera   Cicadidae
Clover weevils   Coleoptera   Curculionidae
Cockroach Orthoptera   Blattidae
Codling moth   Lepidoptera   Olethreutidae   Carpocapsa pomonella L.
Cone worms Lepidoptera
Corn earworm   Lepidoptera   Noctuidae   Heliothis zea (Boddie)
Cotton boll weevils Coleoptera   Curculionidae
Crabs   Crustacea

61

Crane flies	Diptera	Tipulidae	
Crayfish	Crustacea		
Crickets	Orthoptera	Gryllidae	
Culicine mosquitoes	Diptera	Culicidae	
Cutworm moths	Lepidoptera	Noctuidae	Agrotis sp.
Daddy long legs	Phalangida		
Damselflies	Odonata		
Dragonflies	Odonata		
Dung beetles	Coleoptera	Scarabaeidae	
Earthworms	Oligochaeta		
Elm bark beetle	Coleoptera	Scolytidae	Scolytus multistriatus (Marsham)
Flat bugs	Hemiptera	Aradidae	
Flies	Diptera		
Flying ants	Hymenoptera	Formicidae	
Gnats	Diptera		
Grasshoppers	Orthoptera	Acrididae	
Grubs	Coleoptera		
Gypsy moth	Lepidoptera	Lymantriidae	Porthetria dispar (L.)
Hairy crickets	Orthoptera		
Harvestmen	Phalangida		
Hawk moths	Lepidoptera	Sphingidae	
Hemipterans	Hemiptera		
Hornets	Hymenoptera	Vespidae	
House fly	Diptera	Muscidae	Musca domestica L.
Hymenopterans	Hymenoptera		
Ichneumon flies	Hymenoptera	Ichneumonidae	
Isopods	Crustacea		
Jassids	Homoptera	Cicadellidae	
Jerusalem crickets	Orthoptera	Gryllacrididae	
Jumping plant lice	Homoptera	Psyllidae	
Katydids	Orthoptera	Tettigoniidae	
Ladybird beetles	Coleoptera	Coccinellidae	
Leaf bugs	Hemiptera	Miridae	
Leafhoppers	Homoptera	Cicadellidae	
Leaf skeletonizers	Lepidoptera	Lyonetiidae	Bucculatrix sp.
Lepidopterans	Lepidoptera		
Locusts	Orthoptera	Acrididae	
Locust seed weevils	Coleoptera	Mylabridae	Bruchus sp.
Lodgepole needle miners	Lepidoptera	Gelechiidae	
Long-horned beetles	Coleoptera	Cerambycidae	
Long-horned grasshoppers	Orthoptera	Tettigoniidae	
Long-legged tipulids	Diptera	Tipulidae	
Lyonetiid moths	Lepidoptera	Lyonetiidae	Bucculatrix sp.
May beetles	Coleoptera	Scarabaeidae	
Mayflies	Ephemeroptera		
Metallic wood boring beetles	Coleoptera	Buprestidae	
Midges	Diptera	Chironomidae	
Millipedes	Diplopoda		

Molluscs	(phylum) Mollusca		
Mosquitoes	Diptera	Culicidae	
Moths	Lepidoptera		
Negro bugs	Hemiptera	Corimelaenidae	
Nut weevils	Coleoptera	Curculionidae	Curculio spp.
Praying mantids	Orthoptera	Mantidae	
Pseudoscorpions	Pseudoscorpionida		
Psyllids	Homoptera	Psyllidae	
Ribbed pine borer	Coleoptera	Cerambycidae	Stenocorus inquisitor (Oliv.)
Roaches	Orthoptera	Blattidae	
Round-headed woodborers	Coleoptera	Cerambycidae	
Sawflies	Hymenoptera	Tenthredinidae	
Scolytid beetles	Coleoptera	Scolytidae	Scolytus sp.
Scorpions	Scorpionida		
Seed beetles	Coleoptera	Bruchidae	Bruchus sp.
Seed bugs	Hemiptera	Lygaeidae	
Spiders	Areneida		
Spittle bugs	Homoptera	Cercopidae	
Spittle insects	Homoptera	Cercopidae	
Spruce aphid	Homoptera	Chermidae	Chermes cooleyi Gill.
Spruce beetles	Coleoptera	Scolytidae	Dendroctonus sp.
Spruce budworm	Lepidoptera	Tortricidae	Choristoneura fumiferana (Clemens)
Stinkbugs	Hemiptera	Pentatomidae	
Tent caterpillars	Lepidoptera	Lasiocampidae	Malacosoma sp.
Termites	Isoptera		
Tree hoppers	Homoptera	Membracidae	
True bugs	Hemiptera		
Wasps	Hymenoptera	Vespidae	
Water boatmen	Hemiptera	Corixidae	
Weevils	Coleoptera	Curculionidae	
Wood ants	Hymenoptera	Formicidae	
Wood boring beetles	Coleoptera		
Wood boring larvae	Coleoptera		

112

Vertebrates Referred to in Text:

Common Name	Class or Order	Family	Genus and Species
Amphibians	Amphibia		
Bats	Chiroptera		
Carp	Cypriniformes	Cyprinidae	Cyprinus carpio Linnaeus
Catfish	Cypriniformes	Ictaluridae	
Chipmunks	Rodentia	Sciuridae	
Chubs	Cypriniformes	Cyprinidae	
Cotton rat	Rodentia	Cricetidae	Sigmodon hispidus (Say & Ord)
Cottontail rabbit	Lagomorpha	Leporidae	Sylvilagus floridanus (Allen)
Cow	Artiodactyla	Bovidae	Bos taurus Linnaeus
Deer mouse	Rodentia	Cricetidae	Peromyscus maniculatus (Wagner)

Eels	Anguilliformes	Anguillidae	Anguilla sp.
Flying squirrels	Rodentia	Sciuridae	Glaucomys sp.
Frogs	Anura		
Gizzard shad	Clupeiformes	Clupeidae	Dorosoma cepedianum (LeSueur)
Gophers	Rodentia	Geomyidae	
Ground squirrels	Rodentia	Sciuridae	
Horse	Perissodactyla	Equidae	Equus caballus Linnaeus
Lizards	Squamata		
Masked shrew	Insectivora	Soricidae	Sorex cinereus (Kerr.)
Meadow mouse	Rodentia	Cricetidae	Microtus pennsylvanicus (Ord)
Meadow vole	Rodentia	Cricetidae	Microtus pennsylvanicus (Ord)
Mice	Rodentia		
Moles	Insectivora	Talpidae	
Perch	Perciformes	Percidae	
Pig	Artiodactyla	Suidae	Sus scrofa Linnaeus
Pocket gophers	Rodentia	Geomyidae	
Porcupine	Rodentia	Erethizontidae	Erethizon dorsatum (Linnaeus)
Raccoon	Carnivora	Procyonidae	Procyon lotor (Linnaeus)
Rats	Rodentia		
Red-backed mouse	Rodentia	Cricetidae	Clethrionomys gapperi (Vigors)
Red-backed vole	Rodentia	Cricetidae	Clethrionomys gapperi (Vigors)
Reptiles	Reptilia		
Rodents	Rodentia		
Salamanders	Urodela		
Salmon	Clupeiformes	Salmonidae	
Short-tailed shrew	Insectivora	Soricidae	Blarina brevicauda (Say)
Shrews	Insectivora	Soricidae	
Snakes	Squamata		
Squirrels	Rodentia	Sciuridae	
Star-nosed mole	Insectivora	Soricidae	Condylura cristata (Linnaeus)
Suckers	Cypriniformes	Catostomidae	
Toads	Anura		
Trout	Clupeiformes	Salmonidae	
Voles	Rodentia	Cricetidae	
White-footed mouse	Rodentia	Cricetidae	Peromyscus sp.
Woodrats	Rodentia	Cricetidae	Neotoma sp.

Footnotes

[1] Scott, Virgil E. Characteristics of ponderosa pine snags used by cavity-nesting birds. U.S. Fish and Wildlife Service, Fort Collins, Colorado.

[2] Scott, Virgil E. [In prep.] Bird response to snag removal. U.S. Fish and Wildlife Service, Fort Collins, Colorado.

[3] Snag or tree use: A: food B: nest C: perch.

[4] Major foods: 1: birds 2: rodents 3: reptiles and amphibians 4: insects 5: seeds and fleshy fruits 6: vegetation 7: other or little known.

[5] Threatened or endangered species.

[6] Wildlife biologist, U.S. Fish and Wildlife Service, Fort Collins, Colorado.

[7] Ecology Department, Colorado State University, Fort Collins, Colorado.

[8]Zoology Department. Colorado State University, Fort Collins.

[9]DeWeese, Lawrence R., Charles J. Henny, Randy L. Floyd, Kathie A. Bobal, and Albert W. Shultz. U.S. Fish and Wildlife Service. Impact of Trichlorfon (Dylox) and Carbaryl (Sevin-4-oil) on breeding birds in southwestern Montana forests.

Made in the USA
Coppell, TX
10 May 2021